VIVE LA PARIS

VIVE LA PARIS

ESMÉ RAJI CODELL

HYPERION BOOKS FOR CHILDREN

NEW YORK

First Edition

1 3 5 7 9 10 8 6 4 2
This book is set in 13.5-point Celestia-Antiqua.
Designed by Christine Kettner
Printed in the United States of America
Reinforced binding

Library of Congress Cataloging-in-Publication Data
Codell, Esmé Raji, 1968–
Vive la Paris / Esmé Raji Codell—1st ed.
p. cm.
Summary: Fifth grader Paris learns some lessons about dealing with bullies of all
kinds as she wonders how to stop a classmate from beating up her brother at
school and as she learns about the Holocaust from her piano teacher, Mrs. Rosen.
[1. Bullies—Fiction. 2. Brothers and sisters—Fiction. 3. Holocaust, Jewish
(1939–1945)—Fiction. 4. Schools—Fiction. 5. African Americans—Fiction. 6.
Chicago (Ill.)—Fiction.] I. Title.

PZ7.C649Viv 2006
[Fic]—dc22   2006041149
ISBN 0-7868-5124-4

Visit www.hyperionbooksforchildren.com

ACKNOWLEDGMENTS

Special thanks to the following dear people who directly inspired or supported the writing of this book: Donna Bray, Jim and Russell Pollock, Maureen Breen, Dave Newman, Esther Hershenhorn, Sharon Flake, and my wonderful parents, Betty and Barry. Also a salute to Sheila, the Foos, Stephanie and the real Paris (the girl, not the city), my SCBWI community, Danielle Spencer, Jerome Kern, Deniece Williams, Blossom Dearie, my friends at Carondelet Catholic school, and to the people in schools everywhere who work so hard to teach and learn about peace.

To Uncle Dave

The world is too much with us; late and soon . . .
—William Wordsworth

1

EXCUSE ME for saying so, but I could not understand why this old white lady was talking to me like I was born into her hands. She don't even know me. I just come for piano lessons, and within two minutes she had offered me:

1. grapes, which were plastic,
2. a seat, on her sofa, which was also plastic and which made an impolite noise when I sat on it, which to me was specially uncomfortable because I am a polite person or try to be, and
3. her advice, which was, I believe the word is, *unsolicited.*

"Don't cover your chest with the book, that's a bad habit. What will you do when you start to get a figure?"

I didn't answer and I didn't move the book because, after all, I did not come to this apartment that smells like onions and yesterday's rain for anything but piano lessons.

"Your hair looks like Minnie Mouse. It's cute. Is that the latest style, that and wearing your pants like they are going to fall down, the whole world should see your *pupik*? Excuse me, I am old-fashioned. So why are you here, again? Remind me. You are selling Girl Scout cookies?"

I sighed. My church closed down. Burned down, to be specific. I could not continue my music program there, so I needed someone else to give me piano lessons. But I did not feel like explaining. "My parents would like to know if you would give me a forty-five-minute lesson once a week." I held up three five-dollar bills like a fan, like Daddy told me to do if there was any misunderstanding.

She waved her hand at the dollars as if they were flies. "I don't need it. I would do it for free, but I don't want you should be ashamed, so I will take the money. And him, what's he here for?"

"This is my brother Michael. He walks me here, and he will sit quietly while I have my lesson." My big brother waved sheepishly.

"How do you do, Michael-who-will-sit-quietly. Wouldn't you rather be Michael-who-plays-outside?"

"Yes, ma'am."

"'Yes, ma'am.' Such a polite boy. I see you have a watch. So go, and come back at four thirty." She didn't have to tell him twice. *OOOOoooo, Michael! Daddy told you real clear to stay here and watch me.* "And you, what did you say your name was?"

"Paris McCray," I said, all tight-lipped.

"Paris?" asked Mrs. Rosen. "What's your brother's name? London?"

"It's Michael," I reminded her.

"Oh, yes. 'Michael-who-plays-outside.' But you, you're Paris. Like Paris, the city?"

I shrugged. "Yes, maybe like the city, but I have never been there to know for sure."

"Do you want to know?" she asked.

I shrugged again. That means yes.

She shrugged and shrugged and shrugged,

3

making fun of me. "Me, too. Now, have a grape and we'll get started."

We did the scales for a while and didn't say nothing but c-d-e-f-g-a-b-c, and somehow this brought us closer. So I explained how my mom and dad were planning on going to France but then my mom got pregnant, and since they already had four boys, they needed the money more than the trip. My momma said, "If we can't go to Paris, then Paris will come to us."

I like telling that story because Momma seems to like to tell it to me.

"So you were the disappointment."

"I was not," I did reply.

She shrugged. "Sorry. Don't have an attack. It's just, in every family, there's a disappointment. Maybe it's not you. Maybe it's someone else. Maybe it's one of your brothers?"

I shrugged. I was thinking that c-d-e-f-g-a-b-c did not give her the right to say such things. But my mother says some remarks do not dignify a response, so I didn't pay her any mind. I just told myself sometimes old people's just ignorant, and that is okay because they will die soon.

She clucked her tongue. "Four, did you say? Were they having a sale on brothers? Your mother is some smart shopper. Wait. What's the matter? What's that face?"

The truth shall set me free. "Mrs. Rosen! You are beginning to exacerbate me."

"You don't mean *exasperate*?"

"I don't know what I mean," I admitted, and felt my cheeks heat under a low flame.

"But even trying to use a word like 'exasperate,' that's some noodle you've got cooking in that pot. I am going to speculate that you are not the disappointment of the family. Or am I overstepping?"

"Yes, ma'am."

"Miss McCray. With all due respect, this formality is going to be the death of me."

"Then I'll keep it up, if you don't mind," I said, because I was mad.

"Is that a curse?" She laughed so hard. "I'll make a chopped-liver sandwich, and then we'll get started. You want one?"

"No, thank you." I shuddered.

Mrs. Rosen had sheet music that was so crinkly it was like paper burned by time, all crusty brown on the edges, with pictures of white people in top hats and round faces that didn't look like any white people I see nowadays, they looked like dolls. Miss Pointy says there are such things as Neanderthals, which are different versions of us that we outgrew. I wonder how fast that happens.

Mrs. Rosen asked if I could read music, and I stumbled along as best as I could, slowly reading the notes along the crispy paper. Then I had to slide my eyeballs over at Mrs. Rosen and wonder about her. Did her lips go like that lady's on the music, a little rosebud? Did she have hair that piled up so soft? *Mrs. Rosen, Mrs. Rosen, your hands have vines growing inside of them, long ropes of green and pink rising up under your skin, ooo I am glad I am not white because it looks scary.* Ooooo when she put her hand on mine to tell it to play F-sharp, ooo-ooo-ooooo!

Then she smashed my fingers on the keys, and they played notes that didn't match all at once, and it didn't hurt exactly, because she seemed to be made out of, I think the word is *papier-mâché*, but her big angry was a shock. "What a business!" she howled. "You play like the keys are going to bite. Don't you *want* to learn how to play the piano?" I was concerned she would take my answer personally, so I did not reply. "You play lousy!"

"I'm not used to these songs," I explained. This is true. They aren't even Old School. They are Ancient School.

She got off the piano bench. "Let's not have piano lessons. Let's have Paris lessons."

Oooo, ooooo! My parents were not paying fifteen dollars for forty-five minutes of anything but piano lessons, and I had to think real fast to see which one of us was going to get in more trouble, me or her. But Mrs. Rosen had already gotten out a book as thick as the Yellow Pages, and it said *French Dictionary*.

"Do you know any French?" she asked.

"Yes," I said. "I know *Poitier*."

"Sidney Poitier?"

"No, Miss Poitier. Miss Pointy, for short. She's my teacher. She taught us her name means, 'I'm your teacher.' Or something. And I know *orwar*. That means 'good-bye.' And *see the plate*. That means 'please, pass the plate.' And *wah lah*. That means 'there you go.'"

"There you go," repeated Mrs. Rosen. "You're

practically French already. You're going to learn a lot here, Paris."

Look, old lady, I don't want to learn a lot here. I don't want any French lessons or free advice or smelly chopped liver on rye. I just come for piano lessons and that's all, I wanted to remind her.

But as I have mentioned heretofore, I try to be a polite person.

And polite people have to eat a lot of chopped liver.

2

I HAVE FOUR brothers. Four! Daddy is a drummer, and he wanted to name all his sons after jazz legends. He said the first son must be announced by brass, so Louis was named after the trumpet player Louis Armstrong. Then came Django, after Django Reinhardt, the great Gypsy guitar player who could play with only two fingers on his left hand. Then Momma got a turn and named the next son Debergerac, after the guy in the play they saw the night Debergerac got the bright idea to come on down from heaven and join the band. Daddy said that was fine right there, that he and his sons made a quartet. But along came Michael, after the composer and piano player Michel Legrand (Daddy says you can't name a boy Michel around here). They absolutely did not know when to stop. Which is a good thing. Because then there's me, Paris McCray, number five. "Best for last," my daddy says. "You hear that, you knuckleheads?" my daddy also says. And all my brothers answer, "Yes, sir," because they really are knuckleheads and they know a joke when they hear one. And sometimes when they don't.

Louis is almost done with high school. When he gets home from jazz-band practice he goes into his room and the door closes, and sometimes he calls his girlfriend, and sometimes he plays his guitar, and sometimes it gets real quiet. It's Michael's room, too, but at thirteen, he's no match for a guy with a mustache. He pounds on the door and says, "What are you doing in there, let me in, let me in, it's my room, too," and Louis mimics him, "What are you doing in there, let me in, let me in, it's my room, too," until Daddy comes home and bangs on the door so hard that it's a wonder it doesn't fall off its hinges.

So Louis opens the door and says, "You rang?"

And Daddy puts him in a headlock and rubs his fist into his head, and Daddy doesn't seem mad at all. So Michael gets his room back, but from the look on his face, watching Daddy and Louis, he doesn't care much anymore.

It's probably not a good idea for the youngest brother to share a room with the oldest brother, but we couldn't put him in with Django and Debergerac, there's no room. Where they sleep was really supposed to be just a closet, but the bunk fit, so Momma took off the door and hung a curtain. Now that they are in high school, they are really too big for the bunk beds, their size-fourteen smelly feet rise up on the footboards. But they've always been there, so that's where they stay. Django and Debergerac are so close in age, they look like twins, and they might as well be, because if one gets a mosquito bite, the other one itches. They sit on their bunks and Django makes puffing noises while Debergerac makes up some rhymes about how great he is, and then they high-five each other and talk about how when they get older they will be the biggest rap stars in the world.

"We'll have a limousine!"

"And girls in bikinis!"

"And a private jet!"

"And girls in bikinis!" Django makes some huffing noises, and Debergerac starts up again. I don't know what those fancy girls in bikinis would think of two brothers who sleep in bunk beds, but maybe by the time they are big rap stars they will be a little more impressive.

Daddy makes them learn real instruments. We are all expected to play an instrument, because Daddy says he can sleep better knowing at least we can put out a hat and earn bus fare and a hot cup of coffee. Daddy sleeps pretty well anyway because he is out all night playing the drums, he goes down to the Green Mill on Fridays and Saturdays. He gets studio work when he can, too. I like when he plays with the little brushes that whisper on the skins and say *husha-husha-husha*. I do not mean to be a braggart, but my daddy is *good*. He can make voices come out of pots and pans if he wants to, and furthermore he is a professional, which means he gets paid to do what he would do for free. I have an organ with a headset, and I can read music. Django plays the bass, and Debergerac plays trumpet—but he does not play it very well at all because he can't practice. It's too loud. Every time he plays, the downstairs neighbors bang their brooms on the ceiling and the upstairs neighbors stomp their feet on the floor. How is a person supposed to learn? Michael has not found his instrument yet, though he can play "Greensleeves" on the recorder.

Momma is the singer in the house. For example, as soon as she gets home from the caterer's, she showers away all the sweat of her day and sings what she calls *arias* because, aria deaf? The whole building can hear her, but she sounds so sweet that they don't bang or stomp. Then she wraps herself in her slippery satiny robe and puts on the record player—yes, a record player, because she likes to play all the records from when she was little.

Last dance.
Last chance.
For love!

Oh, she adores Donna Summer. My daddy gets all excited when she starts up, he brings out the disco light he got her for her birthday and sets it spinning. He sits back and watches Momma sing and dance, the colors crossing all over her face and shoulders.

When my parents shoo us out the house, my brothers make a circle around me while we walk for a while, until we get unstuck, and then they sort of wander off and do their own thing. Still, one brother or another always has an eye on me. Sometimes it gets on my nerves, but mostly I don't mind. I'm used to it.

My brothers are very nice to me for the most part, and here is why. When I was about six years old, we were playing in the living room, just horseplay while Momma was in the kitchen, and Momma kept yelling at us, "Cut it out! This gone end in tragedy, this gone end in tragedy!" But I didn't know what tragedy was so I ignored her. My brothers were taking turns holding me under my armpits and swinging me around in a circle. My legs were sticking out and kept hitting things and toppling things over—the magazines on the coffee table and the lamp, for instance. I was laughing and getting so dizzy that when I looked out the window it seemed as if the buildings were slowly falling down, so I said "stop!" because I was too young and dumb to know that when you say "stop" to big brothers, they hear "go."

When Michael finally put me down I couldn't even stand straight, and my whole body sort of spilled forward like I was running down a hill. I couldn't stop myself. I hit my head on the low corner of the mantel over the brick fireplace that can't even hold a fire, it's just for decoration. Then I heard this gasp and all my brothers froze around me, their mouths all open like they were singing but no noise coming out and their eyes as big as I had ever seen. So I said, "What?" and then I had to blink because something wet was in my eye. I wiped it and when I took my fingers away, there was the red-brown of blood. I started screaming so high I couldn't even hear myself, and Momma came running in, still holding her dish towel.

"Michael kilt the baby!" Django shrieked, and soon they were all shrieking and hopping and pulling their own hair, but Momma didn't shriek, she just pressed that dish towel to my head and scooped me up like I really was a baby. She threw open the front door so hard it banged, and she didn't even bother to close it after her, she just ran down the stairs and all the boys followed. She started trying to flag down a car to take us to the hospital. Finally a truck stopped, but there wasn't enough room in the front seat for five kids, so the boys had to stay and wait for Daddy and *behave*. Even though I was pretty sure I was dead, I still remember seeing them through the half-open window, all on the stoop looking so worried and sorry. The driver delivered us to Children's Memorial Hospital. Momma offered the man five dollars for driving, and he said no, and then she said please, please take it, and so he said okay. Momma spent the rest of the time in the waiting room blotting my bloody head with the dish towel and talking under her breath about "When you grow up don't you marry a man who takes five diggity dollars, excuse my language, from a woman with a bloody baby on her hands, you just don't *do* that, see, it doesn't *matter* if it's being offered, that's not a *gentle*man, your own father would have *never* taken five dollars off a woman in need in a million years, so you just see to it that you don't get yourself mixed up with the likes of that truck driver when you're grown, you just wait for the right person." She said a lot of other words, too, but as I have mentioned, I am a polite person and so I will not repeat them.

I got six stitches.

When I came home, my brothers were in the living room real quiet, like it was church, and Daddy was there, too, looking as mad as hot sauce. All the boys looked relieved and stood up to run to me, but Daddy ordered them to sit down. He looked like the last thing he said was still rattling the tonsils inside his mouth, and he narrowed his eyes at my brothers like they were the dirtiest dogs in the world. He picked me up in his arms and gave me an Eskimo kiss and whispered, "How's my princess?"

I knew Daddy had yelled at them real good and I had missed it, so I tried to smile extra sweet as to inspire an encore. "I got stitches in my head, Daddy."

"I know, baby, I know." He kissed my forehead and I winced. "You see that!" He roared at the boys. "Now we can't even kiss the baby! Now we can't! Even kiss! The baby! Now what do you say to your sister that you almost killed!"

"Michael did it," said Louis, real low.

"And you weren't all playing?" Daddy growled. "I know how it go."

Louis crossed his arms and his legs and clucked his tongue and stuck out his lower lip, but his eyes were wet. Debergerac and Django were wiping their noses on their sleeves. Michael took the thumb he was biting out of his mouth and said, "I'm really sorry, Paris."

"Calm down," said my mother. "Y'all can still kiss her. You just can't wave her around like a flag." She took me out of my father's arms and made me stand up. "You help me in the kitchen. The living room with these wild boys is no place for you."

So I followed her to the kitchen. But it seems like since that day I never really came out. For instance, since that day I never felt like I'm flying and I never knocked over a lamp. From then on, I always knew I was the girl and they were the boys. I still have a little scar on my eyebrow. The hair never grew back in that one place, and whenever my brothers look at me I feel like they can see it, reminding them, *You can kiss me but you can't throw me around.*

People treat you different once they know you can bleed.

I know that. But I think no one in my family knows that better than Michael.

3

SHE BOUNCES HIM up against the wall, his back hits the bricks again and again. The look on Michael's face is just shock. Each time, he acts like it's going to be the last, and he starts to walk away. But it's not the last. He is almost smiling, because when people are in pain, sometimes their faces go like that. It is a terrible thing to see.

"Okay, that's enough," I say.

"Says who?" says Tanaeja.

I don't know who says—I don't know if I can be the one to say. She and I are the same age, but she is as big as him, and more solid. She didn't used to be mean like that. I would see her at the library, my brothers would take me there over the summer and hang around in the air-conditioning while I would look for books. I didn't talk with her because she would see me standing with my brothers and make an unfriendly face that seemed more and more bent up as the weeks wore on. Finally, when we come back to school, she started picking on him. Not me, *him*. When she feels like it. Doesn't make sense.

I know I can take her, because I am mad enough, but then what? He cannot have his sister three years younger defending him. Django once explained to me real plain that if I step in, the kids on the playground will tell their older brothers and sisters, and when Michael goes to high school next year, they will put his wussy behind in a locker. Debergerac says, "For God's sake, Michael's going to have a hard enough time being beat up by a fifth-grade girl without having his fifth-grade sister sticking up for him." We tried to give Michael a pep talk, but when it comes to fighting, he isn't very peppy.

"Just haul off on her," Django pleaded. "Let it rip."

"We'll teach you," offered Debergerac. "Come on. "See? Put your thumb outside of your fist when you fight, otherwise you can break it."

"Nuh-uh," said Michael. "Not my style."

"Don't waste your time. He's chicken," Debergerac diagnosed.

"Oh, yeah? Was Ruby Bridges a chicken?" Michael was talking about when black kids and white kids went to school together for the first time. "She had crowds of bullies, grown folk pushing her around, and she stood there and prayed for them. So I'm going to be brave like that."

"Come join us in the twenty-first century," Louis heckled. "We're waiting for you."

"You know what your problem is? You watch too much PBS, brother-man," said Django. "Tell you what, if I had been Ruby Bridges, they'd have been the ones praying. I would have throwed a brick at every one of their cracker heads. *Plink, plank, plunk.*" Django gingerly pantomimed letting them fly.

"You won't get into heaven acting like that," I reminded him.

"I'd rather be where they bake the bricks!" Debergerac said brightly.

"Just keep doing what you're doing," Michael suggested.

"Maybe you should have Tanaeja over and knock

her head on the mantel," said Django. "Or can't you stand the sight of a little blood?"

My brothers hooted. Michael turned on his heel and walked out of the room.

"That's the spirit, Saint Michael!" cheered Louis. "Peaceful resistance! Eyes on the prize! You shall overcome!"

"Yes, I shall," Michael called over his shoulder, and then he called Louis a name that assured us he still fell a few inches short of being a saint.

Django scratched his head. "Why don't he have no friends to have his back? Only that white boy who comes over and plays patty-cake with him."

Michael has an occasional friend named Frederick, not Fred or Freddy but *Frederick*, and he looks so corny, like out of a filmstrip. He wears button-down shirts and has glasses like Malcolm X, but he's white, and believe me, on a white boy those glasses got a whole different effect. He cooks in the kitchen with Michael, and get this, he brings his own apron. You can be sure Louis has words to say about *that*, but never to Frederick's face, and he better not, either, because Frederick's plenty nice, whatever else someone might want to say about him.

Michael really likes Frederick, and they never fight. They watch cooking shows together the way some people watch sports, making big shouts when the guy on TV adds a certain ingredient, either,

1. "Oh, man, do you hear that sizzle? That's going to be great!" like their team is winning, or

2. "Oh, no, stop, stop! He ruined it!" like their team just lost and they are mad at the player for blowing it.

"Michael, he's just soft like that," says Louis.

Soft like what? I wonder.

My parents worry less about Michael's softness than Tanaeja's hardness. Daddy says, "I'm going down to that school and give that girl a piece of my mind. No, not her mother, I got words for *her!*" That makes it so Michael doesn't say nothing more to Daddy about it.

Momma says, "Think of Dr. King. Just act nice. She'll get tired when she sees she can't bother you." That hope glows in the evening and fades in the morning.

Sometimes Michael tries to defend himself against Tanaeja, but it's with an open hand and he looks funny. I hear voices laugh, dry and mean, like donkey-braying. It's not enough till someone tells her: Here comes a teacher. Here comes the crossing guard. Here comes someone's mom. Then they all walk away, like the end of a game.

But it's not a game. At night, across the hall and through the half-open door, I see him lying in bed on his stomach, he can't lie on his back because the blades of his shoulders are bruised a deep black and green. If he had wings, isn't that where they would sprout? She bruised my big brother's wing buds, I think. And then I think, I'm going to kill her. I sleep with clenched fists, except when they jerk alive, moving like I am pushing her against the brick wall. *How you like it?*

But I catch myself. Django and Debergerac are right. Michael has got to settle this himself. I can't worry about him all the time. I want to be everybody's little sister, that's all. I want to be soft, too.

4

I DO NOT mean to show off, but I am the president of the Extreme Readers Club. I made a bunch of forms, which include questions such as name, address, age and birth date, home phone number, cell phone number, and allergies (if any). I've read thirty-one books since the fifth grade, not including fourteen full cereal boxes (front and back), the *TV Guide* once a week, and nineteen mail-order catalogs, including but not limited to *Pottery Barn Kids*, which features a canopy bed that I hope to have in the future. I have gotten E's for Excellent in reading since the second grade, and I have my own library card with no books overdue, and furthermore, I come from a family of readers. Django and Debergerac like to read Mad magazine and Vibe. Louis reads the *Sports Illustrated* Swimsuit Issue and the *Chilton Repair Manual for the Chevrolet Caprice Impala, 1979–1989*. Michael likes to read cookbooks. Daddy reads the newspaper's "Weekend" section on Fridays, and when she wants to, Momma reads minds. So it was only natural, for example, that I should grow up to become the Extreme Readers Club president, having been encultivated in such a atmosphere of literary culturation.

When I grow up I would like to be a lawyer and a ballerina, and when I am done doing those things I am going to run a bookstore. I hope it does not hurt my librarian Miss Espanoza's feelings because she has a good job, too, and she says I could be a librarian when I grow up because I have a strong sense of justice, and librarians have to fight for freedom to read. That's nice, but the thing is, I would like a job with a cash register and a drawer that comes out when you total the amount. At my bookstore I am going to have live entertainment so my brothers can play their instruments, and I am going to have a punch card whenever someone takes my suggestion for a good book, and if they have six punches then they can have ten percent off. Or something. I don't know.

But what I do know is growing up takes forever, so in the meantime I suggested to my teacher, Miss Pointy, that I would like to be in charge of a newsletter for other kids who would like to read, and she said, "What do you mean, exactly?" and I told her I wanted to print up something every week that says what book I like, and if they read my book, I will punch their card, and in this way it will be like everybody in my class is in the Extreme Readers Club. Miss Pointy dug in a low cupboard, pulling out tissues that once were smooth and pink but now are gray and smashed into accordion shapes and jugs of tempera paint that are all dried-up powder, and we disturbed two millipedes but neither of us screamed (much), then she took a deep breath and dragged out a machine that was like a metal dinosaur, which she said was a mimeograph machine.

I said, "Oh, Miss Pointy, why can't I just use the computer?"

And she said, "Well, Paris, you may eventually.

However, why don't you try this for fun?" She asked did I know about Edison, who "invented this apparatus" and "furthermore, speaking of history, what about Gutenberg, why, he invented printing" and that "he was able to accomplish earth shaking achievements using even more primitive measures," so according to her, the sky is the limit and the world is my oyster "thanks to this relatively modern technology." I know she was just saying this because Darrell had a tantrum with both fists during Number Munchers and now the one keyboard to the one computer in the classroom is broken, and every time we turn it on it just writes eeeeeeeeeeeeee all over the screen. But Miss Pointy is also a very polite person and so she did not mention it. She poured a blue liquid into a big drum. She said that it was a magic potion, but that's just the way she talks. I told her it smelled good, and she made me promise not to sniff it on purpose, only teachers can sniff it, and then she said, "Ha-ha, just kidding," and looked around.

Then she showed me how to draw on an inky blue piece of paper and stick it into a metal lip on the drum and snap it in place, and then she turned a handle and the machine said *"Kachoink-kachoink,"* and *wah lah!* There were two copies. Miss Pointy gave me a whole ream of paper and told me to live it up because mimeographs are economical. Luz said she would draw the pictures, and Sahara would write the reviews, and I would *kachoink-kachoink* because I was the only one who knew how to use the machine. Miss Pointy said this would be a great service and we could have payment of one sticker each per week, so I do not mean to show off but I guess that made us professionals.

Having a good idea made me feel like that dream where I take one step and float all the way down the block. It made me feel like blue ink rising in me, it made me spin like a mimeograph drum. Soon we would be famous to the ones who know us.

At the library there is a computer, and Miss Espanoza said I could feel free to use it for my project, which gave me a big temptation, but Miss Pointy had already suffered through two millipedes on my account, and plus, I liked doing *kachoink-kachoink,* so I explained that the mimeograph was more economical. Miss Espanoza said she understood, but asked if she could at least help me design a membership card. We printed the cards out six to a page, and there was a picture of a stack of books in full color on every one of them, and they were so beautiful that I almost felt a little jealous of myself. Sahara and Luz helped me cut them out, and we wrote in the names of all of our classmates, which was fun, like making valentines. We could not figure out how to make big dots all the way around to punch on the computer, so we had to draw those in. Luz had juicy markers that smelled like fruit, so we did all different colors (but especially purple, because grape smelled the best). Luz also had a paper punch in the shape of a star, so people couldn't cheat and punch the cards themselves, because I bet nobody else has a hole-punch like that. I kind of wanted to be the hole-puncher, but that's okay, I still got to work the mimeograph machine, and fair is fair.

Miss Espanoza said, "Be careful, Paris, if you recommend a book and there is only one in the library, then other kids will have to wait, and things could go very slowly." Sahara said, "Why don't we recommend an author or a subject instead of a particular book, like maybe Beverly Cleary, because she has books about girls, like *Beezus and Ramona*, and the boys can read *The Mouse and the Motorcycle*." When I have my bookstore, you better believe I am going to hire Luz and Sahara as managers.

Miss Pointy calls a rough draft a "sloppy copy," and so Sahara made a sloppy copy of her article about how Beverly Cleary has written funny books for both boys and girls, and then she gave a long list of titles. Luz copied a picture from one of the covers of her books. I picked out the lettering on the computer for our logo and traced it onto the special mimeograph paper. Then Luz copied Sahara's article in her neat, round handwriting, going so slow and concentrating so hard some of her tongue stuck out in the corner of her mouth. We showed it to Miss Pointy, and she hugged us all in a big hug, and she said she was glad because she had a lot of those books. She pulled extra paperbacks out of her closet, and we stayed in for two recesses to cover them with clear contact paper. I guess the word is *merry*, and I know that is an old-fashioned word, but that's the way it felt, sitting by the windows working together, listening to Miss Pointy's radio echoing in all corners of the big empty classroom.

I am also glad for the Extreme Readers Club because when I am doing *kachoink-kachoink*, I am in for recess, and I am not the girl who sees her brother get beat up on the playground. I am not the girl who thinks thoughts that are against the Bible. I am not the girl who has hating feelings and revenge feelings. I am a polite girl, an idea girl. That's the real me. The one I want to be.

5

DADDY SAYS music casts a powerful spell, and I have seen it for myself. At church, when the choir gets cooking, the old folks can swing. They close their eyes and dance, their feet move and their hands clap, they shuffle and shimmy, and oh my, they get loose, but Jesus loves them how they are, so why should they be embarrass? Oooo, Mrs. Rosen, it's the same when you play, your hands get young again, they skip like children. Oooo, Mrs. Rosen, when you play when you play, I hear the electric buzz of a sign that glows with your name in lights: NOW PLAYING, MRS. ROSEN!

Mrs. Rosen stopped all of a sudden and rubbed the joints in her hands. "Arthritis," she apologized.

"Wow, Mrs. Rosen, you are good."

"Once upon a time." She moved her hands across the keys, sad and loving-like, the way some people's eyes cross an old photograph. "See how you can play if you practice every day?" She started up again with c-d-e-f-g-a-b-c, and I didn't mean to be rude, but I had to tell her. "Mrs. Rosen, I can already play a little. I know my scales."

She looked at me in a remembering way, and I knew she was thinking of our first day, when she had to mash my fingers on the keys. But the nice thing about old people, they can pretend to forget. "Oh, you do? So show me."

I started to play and sing, "His Eye Is on the Sparrow."

I learned that song at church. I love church, or at least, I did love church. I went to the church that my Gammy went to, and even though she passed before I could meet her, I know she wore a nice wide-brim hat every Sunday. When I see the ladies wearing wide-brim hats, I know I have a whole church full of Gammies. You might not know their names but you better know a Gammy when you see one, picking lint off your shoulder and tucking the tag in the back of your dress and licking their thumbs to wipe off the corner of your mouth and passing you a mint down the pew. They flap their fans until it looks like moths lighting in their laps and taking off over their heads. Babies cry and the Gammies turn around and give their advice for free, talking about how "Maybe you need to not stay out so late with your man friend (mmm-hmmm!), get home and put that child to bed at a decent hour so's he won't be cryin' at church (amen!), well you can keep looking at me like that, don't change which way the river flows, now does it?"

Then Pastor Frye would say, "One line of the cross rises up to heaven, but the cross also has a line that stretches out, horizontal, of this earth." He said to serve Him we must do both things: reach up toward heaven, but also reach out to those here on earth. Amen, amen, said the Gammies, because nothing was really true until the Gammies said so. Then we sang, and with every note, together, we built a wall of believing made of musical brick and mortar, hallelujah. Back then, my brothers played the music and my voice joined in the joyful noise, and right then I believed in heaven because I saw a piece of it.

But that church had a fire in the middle of the night. Now when it is Sunday morning, we have to be told to get out of bed because this new church is big and we are lost in it. The boys in the band have already been assigned, so my brothers don't play their instruments most times. There is a big buzzing air conditioner, and I don't smell flowers or hair oil or even other people's sweat and I feel wicked and I think the word Pastor Frye would use is *corporeal* for missing these earthly things.

When the new pastor talks I might as well be watching television because he's so far away and I don't feel like he knows us. He says things like, "Don't be acting one way in church and then walk out the door and treat people bad and then come back like life is some Etch A Sketch that you scribble up on and then shake it clean on Sunday mornings, nuh-uh!" In other words, don't act all nice up in here and walk out and sin. Well, I know that's some kind of baloney sandwich right there because lo and behold in the fifth row is stupid Tanaeja wearing her halo and not looking in my direction, yeah that's right, she better not if she knows what's good for her. She wears the same purple dress with puffed sleeves and rows of elastic ribbon and lace, and it's so high above her knees, I bet she's been wearing that same dress to church since she was eight. Her hair is always done fresh, up in tidy little cornrows with white beads gathered at the nape of her neck, don't she look so pretty, well, well, well, clearly even the Devil knows how to dress up on Sundays is all I have to say about *that*.

So I do not like going to that church anymore, and I am glad to sing His praises here in Mrs. Rosen's apartment that is so tidy, in front of Mrs. Rosen, who is old like a Gammy.

But Mrs. Rosen is not like a Gammy in any other way. I got done singing and instead of saying, "Well, well, Paris, that was very good," or "Oh my, Paris, I had no idea how advanced you are," she said, "Do you really believe that?"

"Believe what?"

"About God's eye being on the sparrow."

"Yes, ma'am." That's what the song said, wasn't it?

"Huh," said Mrs. Rosen. "With all that goes on in the world, you think so?" With all *what* that goes on? I guess I was looking at her a funny way.

"You know, that song reminds me of a story. Something I remember from long ago. Once, when I was not much older than you, I hid in the forest, and what did I see? Well, I'll tell you. A big black hawk fell on a chipmunk who had done nothing to no one as far as I could tell, and all the while, a little sparrow is turned the other way, singing like it doesn't see. *Tweet tweet.* Like nothing. His eye is on the sparrow, maybe. But what does the sparrow have his eye on? That's what I want to know."

Is that the whole story? I wondered.

She patted my hand. "You'll have to excuse me," she said. "I'm sure it is very nice to believe there is some man standing on a cloud with nothing better to do than babysit all the little sparrows and chipmunks."

"Yes, ma'am." I felt myself starting to get, I think the word is *huffy*. "It is."

She shrugged, but her shrugs don't mean *Yes*, they mean *I don't know*. "I guess I have become a bit of an agnostic."

"Maybe an optometrist can help you," I suggested.

"You're thinking of an astigmatism," she said, and laughed. "Maybe God has one." Mm! I had a feeling Mrs. Rosen wasn't a Baptist.

"That's not the way I see it," I said, because I didn't want any confusion about whose side I was on. "I am a witness to God." That's what we say in church.

"Witness, huh?" Mrs. Rosen seemed to move the word and her teeth around inside her mouth, and studied my face for a long, uncomfortable minute. "Well, Paris McCray, I'm glad to know where you stand and also that in fact, you play the piano very proficiently. So since you like birds, I will teach you this song.

"I'm a little jazz bird, and I'm telling you
  to be one, too.
For a little jazz bird is in heaven when
  she's singing blue."

She asked me to sing my song at the same time as she was singing her song, and it came out:

Mrs. Rosen: *I'm a little jazz bird, and I'm telling you*
  to be one, too.

Me: Why should I be discouraged,
  why should the shadows fall?
Mrs. Rosen: 'Cause a little jazz bird is in heaven
  when it's singing blue.
Me: Why should my heart be lonely and long
  for heaven and home?
Mrs. Rosen: I say it with regret, but you're out
  of date.
Me: When Jesus is my portion,
  my constant friend is Heeeeeeeee.
Mrs. Rosen: You ain't seen nothing yet,
  'til you syncopate. . . .
Me: His eye is on the sparrow, and I know
  he watches over me.

She rocked back and forth with happiness when we were done. "Paris McCray, I think you are maybe like me, a little jazz bird," said Mrs. Rosen.

I don't think I am like you, I said inside my head.

But walking home with Michael, I saw a man half asleep in a doorway, with shoes so worn I could see three of his toes. Was His eye on this sparrow? I wondered. It didn't seem much like it. I wondered if

He loved poor people less, but if He did, why would He make so many of them? The thought crossed my mind, too, where was God's eye when the electric fire burned my Gammy's church down to the ground? It did seem kind of silly, some guy on a cloud. . . . I tried to shake these thoughts. Maybe agnostic is contagious.

A car with dark glass windows that rattled from the vibration of the bass thumped by, and we could hear the electric window slide down. Michael let go of my hand, moved me inside the curb, all the while not looking at the car, pretending not to see it pass, though I could hear him sigh when it did. Then Michael took my hand again. And there was Tanaeja on her stoop, looking at us with narrowed eyes.

I hoped His eye was on us, because it felt like a lot of other eyes sure were. And through it all, Michael's eyes were on the pigeons circling in the sky, away from these dark things.

6

WHEN WE PASSED out the first issue
of our newsletter, the *Extreme Readers Club Extra*,
it was in the classroom, and people got so excited
that they got out of their chairs and crowded around
us and grabbed, which was not polite, so Miss
Pointy had to remind everyone loudly about sit
down and don't worry, everyone will get one. Then I
got in front of the room and called names for punch
cards, and everyone was very good, and I
was so excited that my insides felt like orange soda,
so sweet and bubbly. I was the spokesperson for
our club, because Luz is shy about her accent, and

Sahara gets nervous in front of the whole class even without an accent.

"Are there any questions about the Extreme Readers Club?" asked Miss Pointy.

"Can we do it during Read Alone time?" Angelina wanted to know.

"Yes," said Miss Pointy.

"Can we do it during Puzzling?" asked Raphael. That's what we call math.

"Well, no," said Miss Pointy. "Unless you finish your work early."

"Can kids from other classes do it?"

"I don't know," said Miss Pointy. "Paris?"

I didn't know, either, and I looked at Sahara and Luz, who were shrugging with big eyes.

"We don't have any more membership cards," I explained. "Maybe next time?"

"That sounds good," said Miss Pointy.

Sakiah raised her hand. "I have already read six books by Beverly Cleary. Can I have six punches?"

"I read twenty books by her," said Darrell.

Rashonda clucked her tongue. "Yeah, right. Name one."

He looked on the sheet and sounded out, "Henry Huggins."

"Whatever!" said Cordelia.

Darrell thrust his body forward like a cobra lunging, like he would slap her if he could reach her. "Nobody ever believes me. That's why I hate this class."

"How will you know if people really read the books, Paris?" asked Janine.

"I'm not sure," I admitted.

"Maybe your officers can write these questions down and discuss them at your next meeting," suggested Miss Pointy. Luz and Sahara at their desks whipped out their notebooks faster than you could say *secretary*. "But the honor system shouldn't be any problem so long as people are honorable. Right, Darrell?" Miss Pointy smiled her fake smile, and had it returned in kind. "Okay. Last chance for questions."

"Yeah," said Tanaeja. "What we get?"

"What do you mean?"

"I mean, what do we get if we fill up the punch card?"

What a stupid question, I thought, and no surprise, coming from her. *Maybe you want a free pizza, a* trip to an amusement park, a medal? If you got what you really have coming to you, you wouldn't want it, Tanaeja.

"You don't get anything," I said angrily. "No matter how many books you read."

Sahara and Luz exchanged glances, and I immediately felt bad for answering without checking with my friends. Of course, it wasn't for me to decide alone, and the class did not seem happy with my answer, either.

"Well, maybe for the kids who fill in their punch card, we can have a movie," Miss Pointy suggested. This cheered everyone up. "But that is for the Extreme Readers Club officers to determine."

"Thank you," I said.

"Yes," said Luz. "We will discuss it."

"Chess. We weel, we weel," said Raphael, making fun of her accent. Luz let loose in Spanish so nobody else could know how well she told him off, except for that he slunk down in his seat and Miss Pointy raised both eyebrows. Then our teacher looked up at the ceiling and sighed, "There was an old woman who lived in a shoe."

"You don't live in no shoe," said Darrell. "You live in a classroom."

"God, you so dumb!" said Rashonda. "Why they ever let you out the fourth grade?"

"I wonder if they took away the old woman's shoelaces," said Miss Pointy. Nobody knew what she meant, so that was the end of it. Miss Pointy makes a lot of jokes like that.

7

BAD ENOUGH that Michael has to always stay inside and play chess or ask around if teachers need help during recess, now he can't even go to the public park? Tanaeja gave him a bruise under his eye, and I have to say that it boggled my mind that someone would actually put a fist on someone's eye. It seemed to me that we were not even dealing with a person anymore.

We hurried home to make dinner. Momma says that after a day of cooking she does not want to even open the refrigerator and see even one jar of mayonnaise or she will turn to stone, so she makes us breakfast but that's it. Four boys plus me and my parents equals a lot of food, and it is my chore three times a week to have dinner ready. Michael helps me in the kitchen all the time since he usually can't get into his room with Louis in there, so we talk, and I watch him cook. He is a great cook, he cuts carrots like a chef on TV and beats the eggs so hard that they seem to rise up off of the sides of the bowl and say, *Oh, please, stop. We'll be good!* I try to whisk the eggs like that, and they end up all over the place, but Michael just wipes them up with a paper towel and rubs my shoulder real patient-like, and says, "It takes practice." I think that secretly he is my favorite brother. Michael is unhappy sharing a room with Louis. He told me so. He said Louis farts in his sleep and sings off-key to the girls in his dreams.

I thought it would be nice to share a room— everyone else here does—so at dinner I said, "Momma, can't Michael share a room with me?"

Daddy answered for her. "No, Princess needs her own room."

"I'm not a princess," I reminded him.

"Aw, sure you're a princess, Princess. You'll always be our princess. Mwah, mwah, mwah." Django smooched me so I had to punch him.

Louis butted in. "Aw, let Michelle room with Paris. They can sleep in twin pink canopy beds, it'll be cute."

Momma said, "Louis! That's not nice."

Michael laughed and said, "He's right, it would be cute."

Then we all laughed, and I put Michael in a headlock and bonked him on his skull, like Daddy does with Louis, but this seemed to slow his laughing down until he unwrapped me from him, gentle, like a sweater draped around his shoulders. "Well, I guess I'll clear the table," he said.

"Just a minute, now!" Daddy squinted. "Did something happen to your eye?"

And Michael said, "Bumped into a door."

"Bumped into a door like heck! Somebody bopped you in the eye!"

Momma got up and felt it, and Michael winced.

"Don't tell me it was that girl! Don't they look out for you at that school at all?" Daddy moved to the phone.

"It didn't happen at school, Dad. It happened at the park."

"Oh, yeah? And when did you have time to go to the park? You supposed to sit in on Paris's piano lesson and come straight home. When in that tight social schedule did you find the occasion to go to the park?"

Michael and I exchanged glances, and so did Django and Debergerac, because I know they were thinking fast. Django and Debergerac owed Michael more than twenty dollars between them, so after some bargaining, they said for seven dollars off the debt they'd cover for him if Momma or Daddy had any questions about his injury.

"I got locked out," said Debergerac. "So Django rang the bell and told Michael to meet me. . . ."

Daddy leaned forward. "Yes? Then what happened?"

"And . . . that's what happened."

"I don't know how I'm supposed to get to sleep with such a short story," said Daddy. "Didn't you have keys, Django?"

"I did, but I forgot them. . . ."

"For crying out loud, Django, they are hanging right around your neck! You gone tell me you forgot your own neck?"

"We still get seven dollars off, right?" whispered Debergerac. Michael swatted him.

"Daddy!" I butted in. "Why should Michael have to sit there for my entire piano lesson? That's not fair."

"It's not about fair! You think your mother and I are made of money? See, Michael, if you pay attention real close, we'll be getting two lessons for one. That there might look like just some old lady, but one of the guys at the Green Mill told me she was a real *somebody* once. The real McCoy."

Rosen, not McCoy, I thought. Shows how much Daddy knows. Momma was looking down at the floor, probably because what Daddy was talking about sounded a little like stealing.

"So you just sit on that sofa in that old lady's house and soak it in until the short hand is on the four and the long hand is on the six, or so help me!" He shook his meaty finger about three inches from Michael's face.

"I am so sick of Michael being bullied!" I stood up. "You're as bad as Tanaeja, Daddy! You too, Louis! Always keeping him out of his own room!"

"Paris." I think the word what Momma did to me

is *chided*, but I didn't feel like being chided. I shook my finger right in my daddy's face.

"How you like it! Not much, huh!"

Daddy didn't look like he liked it very much.

"OOOoo, Paris gone crazy," whispered Django.

"And stealing know-how from some poor old lady!"

"Paris!" Momma more than chided.

"And you, Momma, you just sit there, talking about Martin Luther King! Huh!" I gathered up the plates, clanking them together in a pile. "See that black eye? That's Martin Luther King for you!"

"OOooo!" Django and Debergerac were hopping up and down in their seats. "Ooooo!"

"You hush up, fools!" I snapped. "I hope your teeth get so mad at you they eat your face!" Mrs. Rosen said this once about her landlady. This made my brothers laugh.

"She's too young for that time of month, isn't she? Though they get it younger, 'cause what they put in the milk."

"Momma!" Now I chided her.

"Don't you 'Momma' me," she said. "I'm just try-ing to think of a good excuse to get you out of the

53

trouble you got yourself in talking to your daddy like that."

"Yeah, now you got to entertain me on the piano," said Daddy. "After-dinner show."

"I don't feel like playing." I pouted.

"Should have thought of that before you opened your mouth to drag Dr. King's name through the dirt," Daddy said real low. Everyone at the table was staring at me, and I felt bad.

"Michael, I am proud of you for solving your problems without violence," Momma said finally. Solving what? I wondered, and from Michael's crooked smile, I could tell he was wondering the same thing. Django and Debergerac passed a look of doubt between them, fast as a silent note being passed under the teacher's nose. "And don't any of you get any wise ideas about taking on that big girl." Momma read our minds. "I mean it. Michael is doing just fine."

"Yeah," said Michael. "See? She only got one of my eyes."

We couldn't help laughing.

To say that Momma don't have to know what's going on in this family is like saying the sun don't have to shine, but this doesn't keep Django and Debergerac from their secret mischief. For instance, the gangs steal things, and in a pinch Debergerac and Django keep them under the bottom bunk until the items "cool down," or people give up looking for them. Mostly hood ornaments from cars. I guess some might consider my middle brothers to be I think the word is *disreputable*. But at least they are dependable about it, and generous with their services to boot. Especially when our parents are out of earshot, watching the TV in the other room.

"We can help you fix that girl," said Django with his big, wide smile that stretches from ear to ear. "We know people." That guy could sell you a bottle of air and charge you extra for the cap, but Michael's not buying.

"No, thanks," says he.

Debergerac leaned up against Michael's shoulder. "Come on, man. Maybe all it will take is a phone call. It'll scare the pants off of her, she's just a kid."

"That's right," said Michael. "She's just a kid. You think Dr. King would have called up fifth-grade girls to threaten them?"

"Dr. King, Dr. King," mimicked Debergerac. "You

sound just like Momma. Look at your eye, brother-man. Seems like we need a new family doctor."

"I'll keep the one we have, thank you," said Michael, and walked off in a huff, which was hard because there isn't much apartment to huff off into. He started washing dishes. Kitchen cleanup is always good for solitude.

I went to Michael. It seemed like he was clank-ing the dishes pretty hard, but when he turned around, he looked almost cheerful. "It's actually a good idea," he said, shaking the water from his hands. "Calling her, I mean."

"What?"

"Maybe if I just ask her to cut it out."

"I don't know, Michael."

"If I ask her privately, maybe she'll stop. Maybe she's just showing off. Get her phone number for me, okay?"

"I don't want to get her stupid phone number," I snapped.

"Well, you don't have to be like that." Michael frowned.

Why do you have to be like *that*? I wondered.

* * *

Then at church that very Sunday, preacher gone talk about how Cain kills his brother Abel in the Bible, and God asks Cain, "Where is Abel?" And Cain gets all snotty and asks God, "Am I my brother's keeper?" like, *How am I supposed to know where he is?* Preacher says we better make it our business to know where our brothers and sisters are, that it is our responsibility to take care of one another. I swear that phony little liar sets up there in the fifth row and cries, she crying so hard and shoulder-shaking so that one of the Gammies hands her up a tissue, and I thought, You *got* to be kidding, Tanaeja, you *better* be crying because you sorry.

So after church I went up to her soggy self and I dragged Michael. She stood there while her momma was talking to one of the attendants, and she said, "I don't know why you got to parade your brother around everywhere you go, Paris," and Michael seemed excited to oblige her, pulling away from me.

I held him tight and said, "What's the matter, ain't you going to slug him here in front of God and your momma?"

"Paris!" She gasped. "This is church."

"You a Sunday morning saint, Tanaeja? Come on.

It ain't ladylike to leave a man with just one black eye. Give him one to match, right here."

I know you are not supposed to say "ain't," but that rule does not apply if you are

1. in Chicago, or
2. in a fight.

She looked at Michael, who was smiling at her that terrible way he does on the playground, smiling like there has been some misunderstanding that if he could just speak her language, he could explain away. She turned her face from us, twisting around her mother like a shy five-year-old. But I caught her miserable expression. So did Michael.

"You see what you did?" he growled, yanking free. "Shame on you!"

"Shame on me?" I gasped. Maybe His eye is on us, but that's all He can do, watch us. Maybe that's why we have to be our brother's keepers. Maybe the caring about each other and ourselves is the only caring there really is here on earth. If that is so, we are in trouble because how are you supposed to be your brother's keeper when he don't even want to be kept? Michael marched off down the aisle, past rows and rows of emptied pews.

The next day on the playground, Tanaeja stormed up to me, and I was sure it was going to be about church, but no. "I read *Ramona the Brave*," she said. "Do my card."

"What's it about?" Sahara asked cautiously.

"You gone ask everyone what the book is about, or just me?" asked Tanaeja. "Do my card, or I'll tell Miss Pointy."

"Go ahead and tell her. We'll see if she asks you what it's about," I said.

"Your club is stupid. I'm going to ask Miss Pointy if I can start my own club."

"You are in our club," said Luz. "Everyone is in the club. Right, Paris?"

"See, that's the problem. What sort of club has everyone in it?" She sniffed.

"And what sort of club are you going to start, Tanaeja? A bully club?" I could hear that bad, hot little girl tensing up inside of me. *How you like it?* I felt my fists clench and unclench.

"Give me the card," said Luz, snatching it from

Tanaeja's hand. Pulling the hole punch out of her pocket, she gave it a quick squeeze over the card. "Okay."

"I read *Ramona the Pest*, too," said Tanaeja. Luz sighed and gave the card another punch. Tanaeja smiled at me and narrowed her eyes. She brushed me as she passed. "Now, where your brother at?" she asked. I didn't answer her, and secretly prayed that he had stayed in to play chess.

"It is kind of hard to have a club where everybody is a member," Sahara observed. "Maybe we should rethink it." Sahara has a lot of good ideas but is not what I would call a "people person," so her wanting to make the club smaller was not a surprise.

"This club is really good. Maybe only people who deserve it should be in it. Maybe the first month it can be everybody, but then only the kids who have six punches can stay in it." Who was this talking now? This bad, hot girl had my voice and my body, but I didn't recognize her.

"Or, how about this? The kids who have six punches can come to a special meeting where we talk about the books," suggested Sahara.

"It's too big," I said. "We need to cut people out."

"Well, Rachel really *is* nearly on my last nerve," said Sahara, referring to her cousin, who was in the class. "She barely reads anyway, just sits in front of the TV and watches shows where they bang each other over their heads with chairs."

"And Cordelia is just a royal . . ."

"Yeah! I wouldn't miss Cordelia one bit."

"No," said Luz firmly. "No! You think you are going to pass out the papers to some of the kids, and not to everyone? Miss Pointy will not let you do that, and me, either. I don't want to be a part of a club where people feel left out. Even Tanaeja, even Cordelia." She looked very serious, almost upset. "No leaving people out!"

"Okay, okay," I agreed. "We won't leave anybody out."

"There's got to be a club where nobody gets left out," Luz insisted. I thought about Michael when she said that, for some reason. "What's the matter with you?" She was almost shaking and could not look at us in our faces. Sahara and I exchanged worried glances.

"You're right," I reassured her. "I'm sorry, Luz. Of course, you are right. I don't know what I was thinking." I put my arm around Luz to soothe her, and this made her wipe her eyes. Sahara and I shared another look, one of embarrassment, maybe not so much because Luz was so sad, but because we both knew what the other one had been thinking: what a perfect world it would be without some people. But Luz was right. A world has everyone, or it isn't any world at all.

8

WHILE I HAVE my lessons, Michael sits in Mrs. Rosen's little living room listening to Bill Evans on her record player. The room has a sliding door so none of us are disturbed by the other. I don't know how he can stand it, waiting for me, but he does not seem too put out. He loves listening to Mrs. Rosen's hokey old jazz records. They used to belong to her late husband, Mr. Rosen, who she says

1. died of corned beef poisoning, and
2. his secretary probably misses him more than she does, but

3. thank God she has his pension, which is why she is able to continue living in the lap of luxury.

By the time my lesson is done, the black vinyl circles are spread out all over her coffee table like plates. Once I slid the door back and caught him dancing on her sofa, with a feather duster as a microphone. It's lucky Mrs. Rosen didn't see his feet on the furniture. Oh, well, as long as he isn't too bored.

But one day, despite I think the word is *protestations*, Michael got shy and left when he saw Mrs. Rosen had a lady guest during my lesson. Mrs. Schwartz was visiting from Florida. She wore black sunglasses and so maybe she was blind. She had a yellow wooden cane and her fingernails looked like they were made of wood, too. But her hair was done up in neat, white curls, and she smelled like peppermint gum. It occurred to me that between the two of these ladies there was probably, what, seven hundred years of life experience? I decided Michael's absence was the perfect chance to ask what to do about Tanaeja's bullying ways.

"To what does he owe this honor of her special attention?" asked Mrs. Rosen.

"I don't know," I said. "She has something against him."

"But what? Does he owe her money?"

"No."

"Is she maybe a little in love with him?"

"No!"

"Then it is a mystery," said Mrs. Rosen. "There must be something about him that upsets her."

"It's not fair," I explained. "He is older than her, and she is a girl, so he won't raise a hand to her."

"I would like to meet this brother of yours," said Mrs. Schwartz. "He sounds like a real mensch. A good person."

I shrugged. "Every day he is pushed around, and all the kids gather . . ." I couldn't talk anymore because the tears were coming.

Mrs. Rosen put her arm around me. "That rotten little *shmendrick* should hit her head once and get two bumps!" she said with feeling. "Excuse me. I know this Tanaeja is just a little girl. But what sort of person makes a show of such abuse? And they gather, you say? Be careful in that crowd, Paris. If they stand around watching a nice boy get beat up and they are not themselves afraid, that means they are of her ilk."

"I think the only thing to do is make friends with her," said Mrs. Schwartz. "Here's what I'm thinking: this girl can beat up the brother of a stranger, but can she beat up the brother of a girl she views as her own sister? Eh? So if you want to protect your brother, make friends with your brother's enemy and convince her to stop." She tapped her forehead.

"Keep tapping, maybe you'll loosen a better idea." Mrs. Rosen waved her hand at Mrs. Schwartz.

"All I'm saying is, it wouldn't hurt to try to look at her through rose-colored glasses."

"What's 'rose-colored glasses'?" I asked.

"It means, looking at the world in a cheerful, optimistic way. Like things are the way you hope."

"Mrs. Schwartz, she brings out the devil in me, and there is no way I can look at her with rose-colored glasses," I admitted. "When I look at her, I just see red."

Mrs. Rosen got up without saying a word. She shuffled into her room and fished around in her bureau for something, and she came back with a red marker and a pair of glasses that had diamonds in the corners. She sat down at the coffee table by the piano with these glasses and this marker and I could tell she was excited because her hand was shaking like a marionette's, just swinging back and forth like she didn't have no control. And then she started drawing on the glass of the glasses and my eyes about near to fell out because! You can't do that! But the marker color was not sticking to the glass so she said, "Goddamn it!" and I raised my eyes and silently apologized, Jesus forgive her, false alarm, it is just an old lady writing on her glasses and all I come for was piano lessons!

She huffed a big huff and said, "So would you go in the drawer in the kitchen to the left of the stove and get me another marker that works?" and I said, "Mrs. Rosen, that is not a good idea, I don't think," and so she started to hoist and reverse herself out of the chair, which I could almost hear like when a truck at a construction site is backing out, *beep, beep, beep,* and I think, Oh, Holy Father! So I said to her, "Never mind, I'll get it," and I got it and she says, "No, a *red* marker," oooo she is impatient, so I RAN and got her the marker because one thing I notice about old people is that even though *they* can't move too fast, they sure get uppity if *you* don't hop to it.

"What are you doing?" asked Mrs. Schwartz.

"You'll see," said Mrs. Rosen.

"How am I supposed to see?" asked Mrs. Schwartz. "Paris, what's happening? What's she doing?"

I couldn't answer because I didn't know. I watched her scribble in the lenses with a permanent red marker, and I felt helpless leaning on my elbows watching her ruin these glasses.

"Hey, Mrs. Rosen, I do not think that's a good idea."

"You said that already," she reminded me.

"What's not a good idea?"

"*Sha*, I'm making a present." So I was quiet until she handed me the glasses, looking as pleased as if she had given me a pearl necklace. "Here you go. I made her rose-colored glasses." Mrs. Rosen talked loud, like Mrs. Schwartz was deaf as well as blind.

"Ahhh!" Mrs. Schwartz clapped her hands together. "Mazel tov. Now, whenever you look through those lenses, you'll see *la vie en rose*, the world the way it should be. You'll see Paris in springtime!" I looked through the lenses and well, well, I did not know the city of Paris looked like a red fun house, all swirled and bulging, and oooo, my stomach.

Mrs. Rosen got up and moved to the piano bench and took out sheet music and played a song that goes "I Love Paris in the Springtime."

"Someday a man will sing this to you," she said. I guessed that man would be about a hundred years old. "I lived in Paris, you know. In 1939." Mrs. Rosen laughed a little. It must have sounded like a long time ago, even to her.

I didn't want to hurt her feelings, but I moved her present up on top of my head and explained, "Mrs. Rosen, rose-colored glasses are hard to see out of."

"You're not kidding," said Mrs. Rosen. "But speaking of *la vie en rose.*" She turned to her friend. "We're supposed to have piano lessons, but for variety, sometimes we're having Paris lessons so she should learn to be Parisian."

"Oho!" Mrs. Schwartz perked up. "That's handy. Did you teach her to dance the cancan?"

"What, you want I should have heart failure?"

"Well, she can't very well go to Paris and not know how to cancan. I'll give directions!" She leaned her cane against her leg so she could talk to me with both hands. "Stand up and hold the hem of your skirt."

"She's not wearing a skirt," said Mrs. Rosen.

"She's half naked? Why, she's practically Parisian already!"

"No, no, no, no, no. She's wearing pants."

"I thought you said she was a girl," said Mrs. Schwartz. Mrs. Rosen got an apron for me and tied it around my waist a little too tight. "So, where were we? Take the bottom of your skirt in both hands, and make so the skirt goes one way and then the other. Left, right, left right. Get it?"

"Now. Pick up one foot, bend at the knee. Shake that foot like there is a squirrel hanging on to your big toe and you're trying to shake it off. Now a little faster. The squirrel is not taking a hint. Kick it off! Kick it off! Now do the other foot."

"Paris, do the skirt, don't forget, the skirt at the same time."

"In a circle! In a circle!"

"You're forgetting the skirt again, Paris! Just leave it in your hands! Don't let it go!"

"Now kick your legs behind you! One, two, one, two!"

I took enough orders for a whole army, and was breathing big breaths.

"Okay! One more time!" shrieked the women.

They sang, "The Night They Invented Champagne."

When we were done, Mrs. Schwartz asked, "Have you ever tasted champagne?"

"No, ma'am." I was still gasping.

"You mean you are teaching her from Paris and you haven't given her champagne?" Mrs. Schwartz accused.

"Shame on me," said Mrs. Rosen. She hobbled into the kitchen.

"So do you like the cancan? As good as your huckle-buck or whatever you kids are dancing these days?"

"Yes, ma'am." I was too winded to argue.

"When you go to Paris, you have to go to the Lido on the Champs Élysées. But wear a skirt," advised Mrs. Schwartz. "Have your gentleman buy you a bottle of the finest champagne and make a toast to the little old ladies who taught you the cancan. Will you remember?"

"Uh-huh," I gasped. If I live.

Mrs. Rosen came in with three fancy, thin-stemmed glasses filled halfway with bubbly liquid on a tray. "Alors," she said. "That's French for, 'bottoms up.'"

"Mrs. Rosen, I'm only eleven."

"*Ça va.* That's okay. In France, the babies drink champagne from bottles."

"*Oui, c'est vrai,*" agreed Mrs. Schwartz. "Do you get a container of milk at lunch? Well, in Paris, the children get a little bottle of wine with a plastic corkscrew. Everyone there eats dessert first or they don't get any dinner."

"You're kidding," I said, almost spilling my glass.

"And did you know, if a Parisian citizen passes a poodle on the street, they must stop and bow? The men kiss your hand to say hello, all of the women have ruffles on their underwear, and children keep balloons as pets. And do you know why they call it the City of Lights?"

"Because it has a lot of lights?" I guessed.

"What they teach in schools these days, you could fit in a thimble," snorted Mrs. Rosen.

"It is called the City of Lights because every morning, just before the sun rises, the French government sets off five thousand fireworks as a national alarm clock," Mrs. Schwartz explained. "Five thousand fireworks, every one as golden as the sun, to commemorate Louis the Fourteenth, King of France, known as the Sun King. The idea was to re-create the sun in his honor, and to wake the city in a spirit of pride unequalled anywhere on the globe. Like the sun, these fireworks create such a blaze in the sky that you would go blind if you were to stare at them directly."

I was suspicious. "You're making that up."

Her voice got low. "How do you think I lost my eyesight?" I looked to Mrs. Rosen, but she was staring at the ceiling and shaking her head. I couldn't believe my parents named me after such a crazy place, though it did explain why they were so excited to have a gander for themselves. "And so, ladies, *chin-chin*! I would like to propose a toast to Paris, both the city, and the girl."

"To Paris, and to good health," said Mrs. Rosen.

"And to the first sip of sweet champagne," said Mrs. Schwartz.

"And the Eiffel Tower," said Mrs. Rosen.

"And the Napoleonic defeat at Waterloo," said Mrs. Schwartz.

"And the steps of Montmartre." Mrs. Rosen raised an eyebrow as well as a glass.

"And Toulouse-Lautrec," said Mrs. Schwartz. "What a guy."

"Are you just trying to get the last word?" asked Mrs. Rosen.

"Who, me?"

"To crepes," I decided to contribute.

"Okay, to crepes," agreed Mrs. Schwartz, "and blintzes, and blinis, and pancakes all over the world. May they live together in peace despite their differences."

"All right, already." The women clicked glasses with each other and then with me.

I felt the bubbles tickle the underside of my nose. I closed my eyes and took a sip.

"Is this ginger ale?" I asked.

"Is she drunk yet?" hollered Mrs. Schwartz.

"Almost." Mrs. Rosen sipped from her own glass.

"'Cause this tastes just like ginger ale," I repeated.

"*Sha*," said Mrs. Rosen, which is how she tells people to be quiet.

I lowered my rose-colored glasses over my eyes and squinted at the two old women through the scribbled lenses. It made me feel good that Mrs. Rosen had a friend, even if she lived far away and she probably didn't get to see her very often. Maybe on Mrs. Rosen's birthday, Mrs. Schwartz sends her a card from Florida. It's good to have friends, I thought. Maybe Tanaeja should be my friend. I let my eyes relax, and tried to picture Tanaeja in a rose-colored dress, smiling, holding a book. I pictured her in a circle of friends, with Luz and Sahara and me.

And Michael.

The picture blurred.

I put the glasses back on the top of my head. Friends with Tanaeja? It must have been the ginger ale talking.

9

MISS POINTY says our greatest export besides garbage is entertainment, so as good Americans we should know the difference between entertainment and garbage. To teach us the difference, she started showing us movies in class. She said if we kept up as a class with the Extreme Readers Club, she'd give up whole afternoons and we'd set up our chairs like a little theater. Miss Pointy taught us camera words like *pan, fade, cutaway,* and *close-up*. She said, "We're going to have a film festival, and if anyone asks, tell them it is cultural literacy." You'd think that would be fun. The popcorn is fun.

The rest is not. I don't know where she finds these movies—she must have to blow the dust off of them, they are so old. They are so old, the gangsters wear suits. They are so old, women wear skirts. The people talk so fast, like in *Bringing Up Baby*, *You Can't Take It with You*, and *Auntie Mame*, or they don't talk at all, like in *The Gold Rush*. Or, worst of all, instead of talking, they start singing for hardly any reason at all. Some guy puts up an umbrella and starts splashing in a puddle. "I'm singing in the rain!" he says. A grown man!

Dominique squirmed. "This is kind of embarrassing to watch."

"Why? He's doing the thing that makes him happy." Miss Pointy shrugged. "Don't ever be ashamed to be happy in front of people. That's your star quality."

One afternoon she showed us *Captains Courageous*.

"Black people's stupid in these movies," Darrell complained.

"Black people aren't stupid. The black people in this movie are *acting* stupid, because the writers were stupid and gave them stupid parts."

"Were the writers white?"

"Yep."

"Ha-ha, white people are stupid."

"They were ignorant," Miss Pointy explained. "The writers probably didn't even know any black people, because they were segregated; you know, they couldn't even sit next to each other properly on the bus, let alone be friends and have lunch together. For heaven's sake, how are you supposed to make a decent movie and not even have lunch together?" Miss Pointy rolled her eyes. "When you write screenplays, you won't be so ignorant, Darrell. You'll show people more realistically."

"I sure will! I'll make white people stupid like they made me."

"You're not stupid," said Miss Pointy. "You do your work and show them so."

"Can't I ever disrespect something without you making work for me?"

"No," said Miss Pointy. "If you see something is broken and you don't try to fix it, you're lazy."

Darrell stood up. "She call me lazy! You hear that! Y'all are witnesses! First she show movies where black folk don't do nothing but cook and clean, and then she gonna go and call me lazy!"

"I didn't call you lazy." Miss Pointy shuffled some papers, unruffled. "I say you are lazy *if* something is broken and *if* you don't try to fix it. Is that you?"

"How I'm 'posed to fix anything when I don't even have a *camera*," Darrell sneered.

Miss Pointy didn't stop shuffling papers, and she didn't change her expression, but she did glance up at Darrell.

"Darrell, would you be quiet?" said Cordelia. "If you don't like the movie, go somewhere else so the rest of us can watch in peace."

"If you like this trash, you a chump."

Kiarre threw a piece of popcorn. "*You're* the chump."

"Please don't throw popcorn," said Miss Pointy.

"You didn't complain when Miss Pointy showed *Some Like It Hot.* Oh, no, you all quiet then. You just mad because Marilyn Monroe isn't in *Captains Courageous.*" Rashonda wrinkled her nose.

"Well, I'm not watching this old-timey *racism*," grunted Darrell, and turned his desk around.

"Well, I'm going to watch, and I'm watching

from the front row, where my great-grandma never got to watch! Look at me, G.G.! We come a long way!" Rashonda yelled to heaven.

"Both perfectly valid choices," said Miss Pointy.

Darrell mumbled something under his breath, I can only guess what.

The next day, in front of the class, Miss Pointy lent Darrell a video camera.

"That's favorites!" complained Dominique.

"True," agreed Miss Pointy. "Darrell is my favorite pain-in-the-behind. He has been working hardest at it. Congratulations, Darrell."

"I'm a pain, too!" whined Raphael.

Miss Pointy shook her head. "Please, Raphael. This is the big leagues. I am loaning it to Darrell, and Darrell, I do it in front of the class because if you break it, sell it, lose it, or do anything else that makes it so it is not returned to me in the same good condition at the end of the year, I will kill you."

"You don't know how to kill anyone," Darrell pointed out.

"But I can read. I could find out in a book," said Miss Pointy.

"Threatening a student is not very professional," Cordelia sneered.

"You're right, Cordelia. Neither is lending him my personal property. But Darrell needs a camera, and I need to kill him if he breaks it. Which," Miss Pointy added, "he won't."

"'Course not!" Darrell was mad at Cordelia. "What do you think I am? She ain't never gonna need to kill me, which is good, 'cause I'd just kill her back."

"Thank you . . . I guess," said Miss Pointy.

It turned out that Darrell was serious about taking care of the camera—and his own behind—because Darrell never took the camera out of the classroom. His front-row seat, where Miss Pointy could keep an eye on him, was convenient because he could plug the camera into the wall and wouldn't run off the battery. At first everybody made faces at the camera, but as the days passed, Darrell and his camera became less interesting. He wasn't even saving anything. When he came to the end of the tape, we would hear the whirring as he rewound it and started over again.

"What are you making a movie of, anyway?" asked Ernie.

"Black people working."

"Good thing you're not in the shot," said Janine.

It did seem like he was up to the usual, not doing his assignments, looking at us, only he had a camera now, and he didn't have as many of what the teachers call "outbursts." He was quiet, except when he finished a tape he would announce the title. *"The Lives of Children of Color, Volume One: A Darrell Sikes Joint." "Teacher Gives Too Much Homework, Starring Miss Pointy: A Darrell Sikes Joint." "Better than Captains Courageous: A Darrell Sikes Joint."*

"Your movies is stupid," said Rashonda after the announcement of *Would You Please Send Jesus to the Office for Early Dismissal: A Darrell Sikes Joint.*

"How do you know? You never even seen them," Darrell defended himself.

"What do you mean? I see the same things you do every day," said Rashonda.

"Not through the camera," said Darrell.

"So you have a machine in your face! So what!"

This conversation inspired what Darrell felt was his masterpiece: *"Rashonda Is the Stupid One: A Darrell Sikes Joint."* It took a full day to shoot, during which Darrell only filmed Rashonda, getting

82

madder and madder as the day wore on.

"Miss Pointy!" Rashonda finally shrieked. "Make him stop!"

"Can't stop art." Miss Pointy shrugged.

I don't know about art, but you sure couldn't stop Darrell.

I had an idea. I said, "Hey, Darrell. I got something you can take a movie of. Tanaeja beats up my brother during recess. Why don't you take a movie of it, and I can show it to Miss Pointy for evidence?"

"Yeah, and I can call it *Paris Is a Tattletale*: A *Darrell Sikes Joint*. I can see it in lights!"

"No, Darrell. I don't want anyone to know it was my idea."

"How come?"

"Because . . . it's complicated," I said. "Just because."

"I seen her do that. Why don't your brother just beat her up? 'Cause he's a punk, that's why," said Darrell. "If a girl started up on me like that, I'd give her a taste of my fists of steel. Hi-yah! Hah!" Darrell did some sad karate chops into the air. Then he started licking some old candy off his fingers. I realized that asking Darrell was probably not one of my best ideas. "Then again. It could be like *Godzilla Versus Mothra.*" He rubbed his chin. "Your brother is like Mothra. Or maybe Madame Butterfly. Tra la la la la!"

Ugh, I could not wait to get to France, where the boys would kiss my hand. "Forget about it, Darrell. Forget I said anything."

10

MISS POINTY SAID we could stay in from recess and have an Extreme Readers Club meeting, and Luz suggested anyone could come. So we announced it in class. Most kids didn't want to miss recess, but Ernie wanted to and Boris did, too, because he does everything that Ernie does. Rachel raised her hand because Sahara would be there.

I know Mrs. Schwartz said I should try and make friends with Tanaeja, and I meant to. I even turned around to ask her if she would please please join us—but when I saw her looking as friendly as a stomach virus, it was just too much. So instead, I turned the other way and asked Tanaeja's friend Janine if she wanted to come. She seemed surprised that I asked, but she smiled and said, yes. It worked just like Boris and Ernie. Right away Janine signaled to Tanaeja to come, too, and Tanaeja raised her hand. I was glad. It felt phony enough asking Janine.

At the meeting, Sahara said, "I was thinking. I am always running out of things to read, and I have so many books around the house that I've finished." Tanaeja and Janine exchanged looks like, *What a nerd.* "I was thinking, I bet I'm not the only one." Tanaeja and Janine exchanged another look like, *Oh yes you are.* Ooooo, oooo. I had to remind myself that I could not read other people's minds. Remember the rose-colored glasses, I told myself. Maybe they are thinking, *Oh my, yes, amen.* I felt a very fake smile starting to plaster itself onto my face, cracking dimples on my cheeks.

"So I thought, why don't we have a book swap?" Sahara went on. "Like, everyone bring in their old books, and we trade with each other. If you bring three books, you get three tickets. Then you trade those tickets for books."

"Sahara, that's a great idea," I told her, which I

thought it was. "Could we trade cookbooks?" I asked.

"How about comics?" asked Ernie.

"I got an idea," said Janine. "We could have different tables for, like, cookbooks, pet stories, adventure stories, all that."

I did not know Janine was also an idea girl. "That's a good idea," I said. Tanaeja gave me a look like, *You think everything's a good idea.* So what if I do?

"I can make the signs," said Luz. "I have new markers where one color can write over another color."

"Cool," said Boris. Tanaeja looked at me like, *You gonna say "good idea"?* I didn't say anything. So there! I could tell her later. I got out some paper to write down our ideas.

"Do you think we'll have enough books?" asked Sahara.

"Maybe we could invite other classes," suggested Janine. "We could have a ton of books."

I started writing down room numbers. If there are two fifth-grade classrooms, three fourth-grade classrooms, two sixth-grade classrooms, about thirty kids in each room . . . I glanced up, trying to figure out how many kids that would be.

Tanaeja was giving me a dirty look. "Quit looking at me like that," she said to me.

"What are you talking about? You're looking at *me*. I'm too busy to be looking at *you*."

"She is not looking at you any special way." Luz stuck up for me. "It is the scar in her eyebrow."

"Butt out," said Tanaeja to Luz.

Ooooo, oooo, keep talking to my best friend like that, watch what happens, I thought. Miss Pointy glanced up from her papers in our direction.

"But maybe we shouldn't invite, like, the kindergarten." Janine was in full thinking mode. "We don't want baby books."

"But boys like books with pictures," said Ernie, and Boris nodded.

"They are also helpful if you are just learning English," said Luz, who had decided to ignore Tanaeja.

"The thing is, there's, like, over two hundred kids in just the middle grades," I explained. "Maybe we should just invite the other fifth grades for starters, and furthermore, we can tell them they can bring picture books, too, like, for their little brothers and sisters, for example, so nobody feels bad."

"*Furthermore*, for *example*," sneered Tanaeja.

I narrowed my eyes. "For example, what? Got something to say, for example?"

"For example, what if someone doesn't have any books to swap at all?" asked Tanaeja.

We were silent for a moment. "I guess then they can't be in the swap," said Rachel. "I mean, it's like, if you don't have a quarter on bake sale day, you don't get a cupcake. Those are the breaks."

"Or your friend lends you a quarter," said Ernie.

"Yeah, Tanaeja," said Janine. "If you don't have a book, I have an extra."

"I wasn't talking about me," said Tanaeja. "Are you saying I don't read? That I don't have books in my house?"

"No," said Janine. "No! I mean, I don't know, Tanaeja, it kind of sounded like you didn't have a book."

"Well, I do! I was thinking of others."

I gave Tanaeja a look like, *Yeah, right*, and Tanaeja sure read *that* like a book. "My eyebrow," I said innocently.

"I think this stupid club is coming between our friendship," said Tanaeja.

"What are you talking about?" Janine laughed. "We've been at this meeting for, like, fifteen minutes."

Tanaeja stood up. "Well, I want to go." Janine looked at the floor, *So go, then*. "I really need a friend right now. As you know." What does a Goliath need a friend for? I wondered.

Janine sighed and got up. "Sorry, guys." They headed out for the rest of recess.

"You have good ideas," said Luz. "Thanks for coming." Janine smiled a blue, sad smile as Tanaeja dragged her away.

"Hey, Tanaeja," I called, feeling brave in my circle of friends, brave with Miss Pointy at her desk. "Lay off my brother while you're out there." Tanaeja turned around. "Maybe you should consider picking on someone your own size."

"Like you?" Tanaeja put her hand on her hip.

Miss Pointy looked up from her papers. "Is there a problem?"

"No, ma'am," I said.

* * *

The next issue of the *Extreme Readers Extra* had a bookmark Luz designed that you could cut out, and that was a big hit.

"Tanaeja told me, 'Great job,'" Luz reported.

"Well, why wouldn't she?" I asked. "You're a star."

"It gives me the creeps," said Luz. "She's been nice to me all week."

I smiled and hid my secret thought, *She's trying to steal you, like how she thought I was trying to steal Janine. Was I trying to steal Janine?*

"Give her a break," said Sahara. "She's got something going on."

"Yeah," said Rachel. "Didn't you hear her tell Janine that she needs a friend right now?"

"She doesn't give Michael a break," I reminded them.

I went to the bathroom. When I closed the door, there was a sound behind me. I turned around. There was Tanaeja, Kiarre, Janine, and two big girls who I didn't know. I felt my legs turn to pudding.

"Hi, Janine," I said. Janine looked at me real sad, like she was sorry for what was coming.

What was I supposed to do? I was completely

91

outnumbered. Can you drown in a toilet? I wondered. One of the big girls grabbed my pigtails like
handlebars. What an idiot I am, I thought, to wear
my hair like this! Why didn't I think someone could
do this to me? I tried to will myself to get angry, but
all I felt was sad. Is this how Michael feels? No, I
wouldn't be like Michael. Don't be soft, I told myself.
There's a time and a place for Polite People, and this
is not it.

Tanaeja was coming at me with a razor blade.
"Let's fix your other eyebrow," she said.

I woke up in a cold sweat.

The next day, Louis picked up Luz and her big sister,
Eva, to give us all a ride to school. "I like your hair
down that way," said Luz.

"I think I'll wear it like this for a while," I told
her.

11

I DID NOT KNOW you could use as many eggs in cooking as Mrs. Rosen does. She took the white wiggly out of each one with a fork and dumped it in the sink, and when I saw them all gathered there in the drain I gagged, but Michael didn't notice. Michael was busy dropping spoonfuls of matzoh ball mix into the boiling water and then *poof*, they popped up like balloons.

"The trick is," said Mrs. Rosen, "you gotta use one more egg than it says on the box. Some people like matzoh balls hard, but what do we know from these people? Better they should melt in your mouth. See here, the bones, they fall off if you've boiled the chicken for long enough; take the whole piece out, cut it into little shmitzie-pitsies. Oh! And a teaspoon of sugar brings out the flavor of the carrots. How could I almost forget?"

Michael's eyes were bright, and though he was not smiling I saw in the line of his mouth, I think the word is *contentment*, here among the eggshells and bundles of parsley and naked raw chicken. I was just following orders, but in Michael's face I saw that he was concentrating, gathering the memory of the order in which these ingredients must parade into the pot. Michael, who has his back bounced against the wall until he bruises, wields here a wide and heavy knife without hesitating, bangs the side of it against a garlic clove with the flat of his hand with the unapologetic confidence of a king who has made a decision. He took Mrs. Rosen's pot holders, which look like little calico hens, and poured out a pot of egg noodles into a colander. The kitchen was steaming, and Mrs. Rosen wiped her face with a dish towel.

"Why don't you sit down?" Michael offered. "Tell me what to do, I can do it."

"Such a boy!" said Mrs. Rosen, hobbling over to

a chair. "Like a knight in shining armor. You must give your parents such *naches*."

"What's that?"

"Pride," said Mrs. Rosen.

Michael chopped the celery and chuckled to himself at a private joke. Mrs. Rosen looked at him hard, like she was trying to figure out what was so funny. I looked at them while I ate sweet noodles called kugel. "Don't choke," said Mrs. Rosen. Who would choke on a noodle? Mrs. Rosen has this thing where she always thinks the worst is going to happen. If you are eating with a fork, she is worried you will poke yourself on the way to your mouth. If you are picking up a few books, she worries that you will hurt your *kishkes*, whatever they are. If you are just sitting still, she hopes the ceiling won't fall on you. I said to her once, "Mrs. Rosen, hey, don't worry so much," and she says, "I worry because I love you, darling," and I do not like this because

1. She don't hardly know me to love me, and
2. When you really love someone I don't think you get such a big kick out of imagining every horrible thing that could happen to them.

This is just my personal opinion, but maybe it is what Miss Pointy calls a cultural difference.

Finally it was time for the piano lesson, for which I had paid fifteen dollars, and Mrs. Rosen played a song called "All the Things You Are" that goes *You are the promised kiss of springtime*, and I sang it. Michael perked right up and said, "Play that again, I like all those sharps and flats," and so Mrs. Rosen did, and then she said, "Now you," so Michael sang it.

"You know what is good about your voice? It is unpretentious. That means when you sing, I know you are not a show-off. It's nice, like Fred Astaire, who could dance a lot and sing a little, and now you, Michael, can cook a lot and sing a little. So, when you come to those notes that are too high, you can just say the words with feeling." Michael did what Mrs. Rosen told him to do while I played the song on the piano. Then Mrs. Rosen went into her bedroom and pulled out a long gown. She commanded me to put it on, and so I slipped it over my T-shirt and jeans. It glinted with sequins that had faded from silver to gray, and a smashed felt rose was pinned on the bosom, which fell somewhere around my second rib. Mrs. Rosen clapped with glee and then got out an old hat with what looked like a pigeon feather and made Michael bend down so she could put it on his head, and then she told him he looked like a black Sinatra.

"You look more like a drug dealer," I whispered when she went to look for a string of pearls. "You look like the promised drug dealer of springtime that makes the lonely winter seem long."

"*Sha.*" Michael imitated Mrs. Rosen.

She strung colored beads around my neck as though I were a Christmas tree, and then she turned off all the lights except for her little porcelain poodle lamp and ordered us to "Take it from the top," and it went pretty well, except for her yelling at me to lift my hands with some *flourish*, but I do not know what *flourish* means.

When we were done practicing, Mrs. Rosen announced, "You are very nearly prepared for your first recital, which will be a performance in front of the esteemed membership of the Myron Levoy-Straussberg Senior Center."

"Me, too?" asked Michael.

"Of course," said Mrs. Rosen.

"Well, okay!" said Michael.

"What?" I couldn't believe my ears.

"Don't worry, I'll let you wear the dress," said Mrs. Rosen.

Walking home, Michael was swinging from hand to hand a plastic grocery bag stretched with the weight of a big container of matzoh ball soup. He said, "Well, that was great. I'm going to learn all the songs in the Jerome Kern songbook." I was carrying the worn gray hardcover volume that Mrs. Rosen lent to us across my chest. "Those are jazz standards, Paris. If I learn those, I can be a nightclub singer."

"Since when do you want to become a nightclub singer?" I asked.

"Well, if I have a restaurant, I can have singing waiters and train them. Or if I'm working in the kitchen, I can come out every now and then and sing a number, so I don't get bored. If there can be singing waiters, can't there be singing chefs?"

Now I understood the look my mother gave me when I told her I wanted to be a lawyer and a ballerina. Michael was humming a few bars of "All the Things You Are," and then he slapped his free hand on his thigh and said, "Well, that is what I am going to sing for the eighth-grade talent show."

Now, for the eighth-grade talent show, our classes file into the school cafetorium, which is the cafeteria with all the tables moved out of the way and a microphone in the middle so it doubles as an auditorium. Some boys do some hip-hop, and some girls dance in matching outfits with their belly buttons showing (which is allowed for this because it is a performance), and they move their hips all at the same time while while boys whistle and the music blares out of a boom box. I did not think that "You are the promised kiss of springtime" was going to go over well at the eighth-grade talent show. "Don't you think that will be great?" he asked.

"I think you are going to get the pounding of your life if you get up there and sing 'You are the promised kiss of springtime' in front of those thugs," I told him plainly for his own sake.

"Even if I borrow Mrs. Rosen's hat?" He looked genuinely disappointed.

I sighed. "Why don't we take it one thing at a time."

* * *

We had to learn a few songs together before we could have an actual recital, and so I practiced on my organ, and Django and Debergerac sometimes joined in. Daddy recorded drumbeats, so when we played the songs it actually sounded like something. The neighbors didn't knock on the floor or the ceiling (except when Django played the trumpet), so it couldn't have sounded *too* terrible.

The senior center had a real chandelier that sparkled with the light from the bulbs inside. There was wallpaper on the walls with white roses, and everyone's hair was a shade of white, except one, whose was a little blue. All this white and light made me think of heaven, except it smelled like bleach and bedroom slippers. I couldn't help but pull on Mrs. Rosen's sleeve and tell her of my admiration.

"What did I tell you? This is a good gig," she said.

Daddy could not come because he had studio work, and when you've got studio work, you've got studio work, that's how Daddy explained it. Momma was working, too. Louis said he had to give his girlfriend, Eva, a ride to the doctor, and I didn't want

Django and Debergerac acting up and ruining everything, so they were not invited. So all who was there was Michael's friend Frederick wheeling people to their places without being asked and laughing at the old men's jokes.

The microphone talked back when Michael stepped up to it, and the loudness of his own voice seemed to make him shy, but even louder was the chorus of women in the audience shouting, "Is he singing? I can't hear," so finally Michael just gave up and really started to sing. On the second song he was warming up and snapping his fingers. He started not paying attention to me and singing too fast, but it didn't matter, because by song number three it was clearly the Michael McCray show.

"Did Jolson just perform, or is that my cataracts talking?" a woman in a wheelchair hollered.

"No, you nincompoop, it was Michael McCray," Mrs. Rosen snapped. "There's a name you shouldn't soon forget."

"McCray? He doesn't look Irish."

Mrs. Rosen waved her hand at her, disgusted. "See what happens when you get old?"

"I heard that," said the woman in the wheelchair. "Watch your feet so that I shouldn't roll over them a hundred times or so."

"Hey, they all talk like Mrs. Rosen here!" said Michael.

"He was as debonair as Cole Porter." A woman with a walker and a floury face spoke like she was being throttled. "And, little girl, I can tell *you've* had piano lessons."

"That's more like it!" said Mrs. Rosen.

Frederick had his arm around Michael's shoulder and Michael was looking so happy, so genuinely happy, his whole face was a wide smile, and he looked all calm and finished, like someone who has just eaten a whole cake.

"Your dad should have been here," said Frederick. "He would have been impressed." And if I thought Michael could have looked even happier, I would say that he did.

"The activity director asked me to come back again," he said. "Paris, are you game?"

"I guess so," I said. I almost said, *If you slow down, you almost made me mess up from singing too fast.* But I decided this wasn't the time.

When we were walking to the car, I stayed behind to hold Mrs. Rosen's elbow and she walked, turtle-like. "Well, I have seen Josephine Baker perform, and I have seen Paris McCray. Now I can die."

12

A T THE SCHOOL library, Miss Espanoza had one book about Josephine Baker, in the Black Americans of Achievement series. I had heard of Josephine Baker. My momma liked her because she was the speaker before Martin Luther King gave his "I Have a Dream" speech, and my daddy liked her because she was a dancer from the jazz age. And now since it seemed Mrs. Rosen liked her, too, saying how she could die now that she had seen us both, I decided to find out about her for myself. Josephine Baker was a performer from St. Louis during the time when black people couldn't drink from the same water fountains as white people and all that kind of crazy. She left America and went to Paris, where she did a dance in a skirt made of bananas and all of Paris fell in love with her. Did you know that

1. She had a pet cheetah that she would take for walks like a dog and a pet chimpanzee that she would dress in diamond bracelets and a snake named Kiki that she wore like a scarf,

2. She adopted twelve children from all different countries to show the world we can live together peacefully,

3. She could roll her eyes in opposite directions, which I could not do even after eleven tries.

I showed Mrs. Rosen the book. If all this in the book was true, it confirmed for me the stories Mrs. Schwartz told that afternoon. Stands to reason, a country that likes a naked girl dancing in bananas is just the sort of place that would wake people up with fireworks every morning.

"Why, look at that," she said. "There she is."

"Did you really see her perform, Mrs. Rosen?" I asked.

"Yes, I certainly did. She was a spy during World War Two, did you know that?"

"I sort of did, it was in the book, but I didn't really understand it." Our history books have the American Revolution at the front and the twentieth century at the back, so we're lucky if we make it to Gettysburg, let alone World War II, though I have learned about Paul Revere four times now.

"Well, that's how I met her. I was in the Resistance, gathering information against Hitler, our great enemy. We needed to know so much: train schedules, names of bigwigs, locations of supplies and ammunition; that's war, what can I say?"

Resistance sounded like the word *resist*, or saying no, and ammunition meant guns, I knew that. But what trains? Enemies? Gathering information? "Were you a spy, Mrs. Rosen?" I asked.

"Loose lips sink ships, Miss McCray." She looked from side to side before continuing in a lowered voice. "Since Josephine Baker was such a big star, and a beauty to boot, she could get into all sorts of highfalutin circles, meet European generals and businessmen whose lips came loose at the sight of 'La Bakaire.' She wrote any information she could squeeze out of them onto her sheet music, using invisible ink. The night I saw her, I was pretending to hold out some sheet music for her to autograph. She switched it for other music, which was coded, and I brought it to my commander. But first I got to see the show."

"What was it like?"

"Ever see popcorn pop? Hot, hot, hot, Paris. Something happens when people see something that new and alive. It reminds them they are alive, too. Oy, the whistling!" Mrs. Rosen covered her ears, remembering.

"Did you see her snake, Kiki?"

"No, not that night," said Mrs. Rosen. "But I hear she kept a whole menagerie in her hotel room. I think some king offered her an elephant, but she turned it down. Is that the least practical thing you ever heard? Where was she supposed to keep an elephant?"

"I don't know," I had to admit. I tried to act like women get elephants every day, I think the word is *nonchalant*, but secretly I was impressed. The most romantic gift I'd ever heard of was when Louis saved up to get Luz's sister, Eva, an engraved bracelet for Valentine's Day. But an elephant? That trumped all. I hoped someday I would be so beautiful that some guy would offer me an elephant. Or at least a camel. I hoped someday I would walk along the Champs Élysées, and lips would come loose and ships would sink at the sight of me. "La Paris! La Paris! Vive la Paris!" they would shout, and then furthermore, I would wave to them from my camel while they took pictures. It could happen. In Paris, anything could happen!

"Oh, Mrs. Rosen, I got to go to Paris," I told her. "I can't wait!"

"So get your shoes on," she said.

"No, I mean really." I laughed.

"So do I mean really. You got something else scheduled?" She opened her closet and took out her coat. "Come on."

I tried to think of something else I had scheduled, for example, but I did not, so I shrugged a yes shrug and got my shoes and jacket on.

"I think maybe we should head south awhile, then east," she said when we were on the sidewalk. "I don't want we should bump into the lake."

"But what about the Atlantic?"

"We'll cross that bridge when we come to it. Hopefully they will have built a bridge by now."

She licked her thumb, held it in the air, and then motioned for me to follow her. "Good thing I brought my cane," she said. "This is going to be a shlep."

"Shouldn't I tell my parents?"

"Listen, Paris, the truth is, some things, parents don't want to know. Better we should send a post-card."

"Mrs. Rosen, I don't even have my toothbrush."

"Haven't you heard? The war is over. You can get a toothbrush over there. Anyway, it's good to travel unencumbered."

I had to agree. Why would you need a cucumber to travel in the first place?

"We'll get you a toothbrush as soon as we get there," said Mrs. Rosen. "And an accordion. First thing."

So we walked. One block, two blocks, and by the third block, I was pretty excited. This was probably the best thing that ever happened to me in my whole wide life. This was one of those days I read about, that starts out like an ordinary day, but then something happens, and the rest of the story is a great adventure. You fall down a rabbit hole, or you climb into a wardrobe, or some old lady asks you if you want to go to Paris. Good riddance, Tanaeja. I'll send for you, Michael. I'll make you proud, Momma and Daddy. Oh, look at that poor deliveryman, those boys in that car, the girls carrying grocery bags—look at how everyday everything is—but not for me.

"Mrs. Rosen! I think I'm seeing things through rose-colored glasses."

"Good," she huffed. "Good." I guess we had walked about six blocks. I looked at her. She walked like she had rocks in her shoes. Her body swayed, and I could hear her breathing through her nose. She was staring straight ahead, concentrating. The coat she had chosen was too hot, and I could see a little band of sweat forming on the highest part of her forehead. We walked another block like this.

"Mrs. Rosen," I said. "I forgot. I can't miss school."

"What's that?" Mrs. Rosen was breathing so heavy.

"School," I repeated. "Don't be mad at me, but I can't go to Paris today."

She stood still, almost panting, until she caught her breath. "It's up to you."

"Well, I want to go," I admitted. "But not today.

Michael has his show coming up. I have to play the piano for it," I explained, I think the word is *feebly*. "And if you didn't come to the show because I made you take me to Paris, I think Michael would kill me."

Mrs. Rosen looked at me hard in the face, her chest going up and down with the effort of catching her breath. "I can keep going, you know," she said, offended.

"I know," I said. "I'm sorry. But I just remembered. I also have to do the Extreme Readers Club newsletter."

"What's that?"

"I'm president of a reading club, and they need me. I print up the newsletter. I'll bring you one, I'll show you." I hated standing there in the middle of the street, explaining things.

"Well, if you have commitments." She sighed, and turned around. "And anyway, we should have brought Michael." She started walking back toward home.

"Yes, ma'am," I said. "Next time, we'll bring Michael."

"But it was nice, being together, just us." She smiled and patted my hand. "I'll get you to Paris another day. I promise. I swear it. You'll see."

"Yes, ma'am."

"We'll go home and have a nice glass of water, you and me. You'll play me a song on the piano."

I smiled. I walked along at her pace, waiting for the day to start feeling like any old day again, waiting to feel like one of the crowd. To my surprise, the feeling never came. All I felt were ginger-ale champagne bubbles, all I felt was a sea of water waiting at some shore. All I felt was that, just by deciding and moving, I, Paris McCray, today came seven blocks closer to the City of Lights than I had ever been before.

13

LOUIS isn't all bad. He has love in him. For example, he really loves his car. Her name is Lala Impala, and he says she is beautiful and requires so much less work than a real woman, but please note that does not stop him from giving Luz's big sister, Eva, a ride to and from the Aldi grocery store, or to the mall, or anywhere else she wants to go.

He teaches me car care. For instance

1. He says a left taillight is something of a formality, and

2. A little rust around the fender don't do no harm, after all it is Chicago and you got to expect a little rust, this ain't Los Angeles, and I say, "Who says it is?" He says, "Don't get smart with me, young lady."

He talks bossy like that because he is the number-two Man in the Family, especially since he earned his car by working three summers at the ballpark. Daddy uses it to get to work on late nights, which he says is a Big Help with a capital B and H. Louis plays pretty good guitar but he hasn't named his guitar yet, so I guess he doesn't love it as much as his car. He says we should treat him nice now, because in one year he's going to move to California, where the cars never rust, and I say, "I thought you said a little rust around the fender don't do no harm?" And he says, "Psssshhhhhh, be quiet, you" in a laughy way.

Well I was thinking how it was sure nice of Mrs. Rosen to get us the gig at the Myron Levoy-Straussberg Senior Center, and how Louis likes to drive, so I told him how Mrs. Rosen is always saying that it's a *shande* that she can't visit her mom because she is way out at Harlem and Roosevelt in Forest Park. Maybe he could drive her?

He looked it up in the *Rand McNally Road Atlas* he keeps in his trunk, and when he saw that it was good and far, he said yes. When he picked up Mrs. Rosen, she came hobbling out clutching her purse and a crunched-up plastic grocery bag. He looked at her twice and asked me in a whisper, "So how old is her mother?"

I told him to hush.

Mrs. Rosen took a gander at Louis, and her eyes got all suspicious. "Where is Michael?" she asked.

"He had a dentist appointment," I explained. "It's just us, Mrs. Rosen."

"Are you here to chauffeur me or to mug me?" she asked my big brother.

"Nice to meet you, too," he said.

"It's better to get these things out in the open," said Mrs. Rosen.

"Just get in the car," he suggested, holding the door. I slid over to the middle of the bench seat so I could be in charge of the radio during the ride. Louis helped Mrs. Rosen into her seat, and even buckled the belt across her lap while she held her chin up and looked at some distant point down the street. He closed the door, and then my brother did stick his finger at me in the threatful way that means "I'll get you for this later."

Well, Mrs. Rosen had the directions written down, and we were driving up and down the big boulevard, and Louis was getting frustrated and said, "I don't know where this place is," and then Mrs. Rosen said, "We're here."

And Louis said, "But Mrs. Rosen, there's nothing here but a cemetery."

Then there was what I think is called a *pregnant pause*.

Then Louis turned in through the gates and said, "Well, Mrs. Rosen, you'll have to speak up and tell me where to go." So he drove as far as he could down a little narrow road going real slow so's not to knock down any of the headstones, and then we got out and walked.

I have only been to one cemetery, and

1. It was full of crosses and angels, and
2. It wasn't so big.

This was like a city of dead people, truly, all the narrow stones lined up shoulder to shoulder against each other, some tall and some short, and on many of the stones was a little framed picture of the face of the deceased, and this made it seem even more like the stones were rows and rows of people. There were stars engraved on the stones and nice words like "beloved" and "dear" and "precious," and the pictures did make them look kind of precious, like the people on Mrs. Rosen's sheet music, only with faces less carefully arranged; that man had big ears, that woman's eyes were close together. Then you looked at the headstone, and those woman's eyes were "darling grandmother's" eyes, eyes that some little kid must have looked into when he skinned his knees. Those ears were "devoted husband's" ears, whispered into by some new bride. Some of the stones said "general" and "lieutenant" and "son" and "brave," and those must have been soldiers. And then on a headstone there were dates so close together, I knew a child must be buried there. I couldn't help thinking about the family gathered on that day, all the tears that must have fallen on that spot of earth. I started noticing that there sure were a lot of kids buried in this dead people city. It made me feel kind of panicky.

Mrs. Rosen was being kind of panicky, too, because she could not find her mother. "I know she's around here someplace!" I thought maybe she would start calling for her, and that would be too creepy. Louis seemed like he was getting nervous, too, but more because Mrs. Rosen was so frantic and moving kind of fast and stumbly.

"That old lady gone fall and break a hip, and I don't know where a hospital is around here," he said half to me and half to the guy whose stone he was standing next to. So I went up to her and tried to take her by the elbow, but Mrs. Rosen shook me off and she almost fell over.

"She's got to be here someplace," she repeated anxiously. "There are so many more since the last time I was here, I'm all mixed up."

"That's okay, Mrs. Rosen," I said. "We're not in any big hurry." Louis flashed me a look, and I flashed one right back. "Is it a big stone, or a little stone?"

Mrs. Rosen looked totally confused, like she might cry. It was awful to watch her, like a little girl searching for her mother in a crowd. "It was right around here. Near a little tree. We're so close!"

I looked around. It occurred to me that maybe a little tree from the last time Mrs. Rosen had visited might be one of the medium-size trees up ahead. "Let's take a walk," I said. I took her arm, more firmly this time, and Louis took her on the other side, and we tottered down the narrow path together.

"Mrs. Rosen, why are so many children buried here?"

"Polio," she said. "Tuberculosis. Let me tell you something. You're lucky to be alive right now," she said absently. Looking around, I guessed that was true. "Where *is* she?"

The path led to a less crowded section of the cemetery. Some of the stones had been cracked in half, some fallen facedown, some with the chalky lettering eaten away by some kind of salt. Vines grew in a choke hold, twining around any narrow decoration, grass grew so tall in some places that it hid the stones completely. A few of the stones had had the pictures smashed in by rocks, or maybe hammers, whole families with faces erased, relatives too far gone to replace them. A couple of stones even had spray paint on them, a symbol that looked something like a Chinese numchuck, all jagged and red. I looked at Louis and he looked back at me, biting his lower lip like he shared my thoughts: What if the stone had been vandalized? What if we were looking for something that wasn't here at all?

"There it is!" said Mrs. Rosen, breaking into the closest thing to a run.

HANNAH BLUHMBERG

BELOVED WIFE, MOTHER, SISTER

SURVIVOR

[then some words in squiggly letters]

1895–1970

I looked at the word "survivor." That seemed like a funny thing to put on a headstone. I thought of that song by Gloria Gaynor that Momma likes to play, "I Will Survive." Maybe Mrs. Bluhmberg broke up with her husband and carried on, like the woman in that song. But it said there, "beloved wife." Maybe her mom had cancer and survived, like all those women jogging wearing pink T-shirts in the park. It was a mystery.

"That's not a tree, that's a bush," accused Louis, looking at the tall flowered thing leaning over the stones.

"Bush, tree, what's the difference?" The color had come back to Mrs. Rosen's face, and she seemed to have calmed down. She searched the ground for three little rocks, and then put them on top of her mother's stone. "One for me, one for little Paris, and one for great big Lionel here." Louis shook his head

and rolled his eyes. "Hello, Mama," she said. "It's me."
She jabbed me in the side with her elbow.

"Hello, Mrs. Bluhmberg," I said.

"They drove me," she informed her dead mother
pleasantly. Then she asked us, "So where is that plastic bag? In it I have scissors so we can trim the weeds
on her grave."

"I don't remember you having any bag," I told her.

"I must have left it in the car," she said. "Luther,
would you go with your sister to get it, please, as a
personal favor? I'll stay here and say *kaddish* and
maybe do a little catching up."

"It's Louis," he grumbled, and took my hand.

Louis doesn't usually hold my hand now that
I'm big, but it was nice, walking through the cemetery together like that.

We came to a big stone:

IN REMEMBRANCE

OF THE JEWS

WHO LOST THEIR LIVES

IN THE HOLOCAUST

"What's the Holocaust, Louis?" I asked.

121

"During World War Two, when Hitler killed six million Jews," he said.

"One guy killed *six million people?*" I was shocked.

"No, stupid," he said. "His army did. Six million and then some." Louis always got A's in social studies and knows many things about the History of the World. "Wait here, I'll get the old lady's bag. Wait here, okay? *Don't move.*" He ran off fast, jumping over stones, before I could say, "Hey, Louis, don't leave me alone in a graveyard."

At first, I thought about the graves that had spray paint on them and that looked like they had been whomped with a sledgehammer. I wondered,

1. What sort of people would do something like that? and
2. Were they around now?

My eyes slid far and near, thinking how good these gravestones would be to hide behind until a little girl like me was all alone, and then you could jump out. "Louis!" I called helplessly.

Then I said nice words to myself, such as *He'll be back in a minute* for example, and turned my attention to the memorial. Six million people is a lot of people. There are only, like, nine hundred kids in my entire school. So how many schools are six million? Round to the nearest thousand, that's like a thousand schools? No, that would only be nine hundred thousand, that's less than one million. So that Hitler guy killed . . . no, that couldn't be right. The bigger the number, the smaller the people became in my head. How many dead people were in this crowded cemetery? It couldn't be more than a million. So six times . . . I looked at the headstones, reaching as far as I could see in every direction. The rumbling sound of trucks on some distant highway was the only thing that was attaching this place to the rest of the world. My head was starting to swim, so I lay down next to the piles of faded roses that were crumbling at the base of the memorial and looked up at the undersides of the whispering leaves, a hundred shades of green, a thousand, six million . . .

I heard a bird singing, and I thought, Who is making that song? My eyes searched the boughs until I found that sparrow. I remembered Mrs. Rosen's story. *Once, I was not much older than you, I hid in the forest, and what did I see? Well, I'll tell you. A big black hawk fell on a chipmunk, who done nothing to no one as far as I could tell, and all the while, a little bird is turned the other way, singing like it doesn't see. Tweet, tweet. Like nothing.*

This bird was singing so hard, such a little thing in the world making that great big song. What was it singing to remember? What was it singing to forget? I looked up at that big marble memorial, casting its long shadow on me. Ooooo, oooo, I thought. I better not be like one of those birds who acts like it doesn't know what's going on in the next tree. I guessed, maybe that's what being a brother's keeper is all about.

On the ride home, we were pulled over. The officer wanted to know why two black kids had a crying old white lady in the car. We told him we had just been to the cemetery, and he looked like he did not believe us. He made Louis get out of the car and frisked him, while his partner checked that Mrs. Rosen still had all her money in her purse and offered to drive her home. She said, "Why would I do that when I have a nice young man to do it?" The

whole thing took about forty-five minutes, with a lot
of buzzing from the police car radio and Mrs. Rosen
saying,

1. "Officer, are we almost finished? I'm *shvitzing* in
   this car," which meant she was hot, and
2. "Paris, honey, is the air-conditioning on?" which
   also meant she was hot, and
3. "Is this air-conditioning aimed right at me? I'm
   going to catch pneumonia," which meant she was
   cold.

I always know what temperature is Mrs. Rosen.

Louis was *shvitzing* a bit himself when he came
back in the car and sighed a sigh that rattled the
windshield.

"The policeman was just trying to be his
brother's keeper," I tried to explain to Louis.

"Well, he wasn't no brother of mine." He put on
the radio to try to relax, I guess, and Mrs. Rosen
piped up, "Is this what passes for music these days?"
and he ignored her. So Mrs. Rosen said, "Let's have
some quiet time." I turned the radio off, and we
watched out the window while Louis drove
the rest of the way home. It seemed like he was

aiming for squirrels. "Slow down," barked Mrs. Rosen. "I just left the cemetery, I'm not in such a hurry to go back."

"You'd come to my funeral, wouldn't you?" Mrs. Rosen asked when we walked her to her front door.

"Of course," I said, surprised.

"When is it?" Louis asked, but under his breath so Mrs. Rosen didn't hear.

"And you would pick the leaves off my grave and trim the grass?"

"Sure," I said.

"And did you see how I left a stone on my mother's marker? Will you do that on my marker? For however many people come, put a stone?"

"Yes, ma'am."

"And at the grocery store, go in the kosher food aisle. There's a little candle, called a *yortzeit*. You'll light it for me on the anniversary of my death?" Louis's expression said, *Oh no, you didn't just ask for one more thing?*

"Yes, ma'am," I said. "And I'll bring flowers and I'll say hello and I'll wipe the little picture with a Kleenex."

"You understand, there's nobody left for me but you, Paris. You and Michael and Mrs. Schwartz who is even older than me (though she won't admit it), and maybe Leonard here."

Louis rolled his eyes.

Mrs. Rosen noticed. She patted my brother's cheek and then handed him a plastic grocery bag by the door that held roasted dill potatoes, a jar of sweet pickles, and a box of chocolates to give to our mother. "Keep the bag, too," said Mrs. Rosen.

"Well, I guess she's nice enough," said Louis when we were back in the car, eating the chocolates.

"That's because you didn't mug her, Leonard," I said.

We didn't talk, but we smiled the rest of the way home.

That night, I lay in bed thinking, my, I do not know if I could do the things that I told Mrs. Rosen I could do, because Waldheim Cemetery is so far away from where we live. This troubled me very much because part of being a polite person is doing what you promise to do. This also troubled me because I realized that I was thinking she would probably die soon, before I would have my own car. If that was the case, I guess I would have to get one of those candles. That would have to be good enough.

14

WHEN I SHOWED Mrs. Rosen the *Extreme Readers Extra*, she made a big fuss. "Who made this? Not you? How can a little girl make a real newspaper?"

"I used a mimeograph machine," I explained. "And a computer to design the header."

"A mimeograph machine! And a computer!" she gasped, and I think I grew an inch. "Why are you squashing down that smile, Paris? You should be so proud! Did your parents faint? I can't believe it!" The thing about when Mrs. Rosen talks is I can't always tell which questions she wants me to answer. I think the word is *rhetorical*. "It looks like a real newspaper, only better, because it has one page, and the other paper, it's too much, it falls all over the place when you try to read it and the print is too small," she complained.

"It's not a newspaper," I explained. "It's a club we started for our class, and this sheet tells them what books we are reading."

"And you see, what you and your friends have started, it will help your classmates to read, what a *mitzvah*, a good deed." She clucked her tongue admiringly.

"Mrs. Rosen, when you were young, were you in a club?"

"Yeeessss," she considered thoughtfully. "I was in a couple of clubs. I was in a club where they put me in a club, whether I wanted to be a member or not."

"What do you mean?"

"I mean, someone made a club where you had to look a certain way and have certain parents, and if you weren't in that club, they put you in another club where woe was you."

This sounded very confusing. "How did you know who was in what club?"

"In their club, they wore armbands and shiny boots, and they all walked together. They had us wear little yellow stars on all of our clothes, and carry membership cards wherever we went. And then . . ." Mrs. Rosen pulled up her sleeve and showed me numbers tattooed on her arm. "Do you know what this means?" She asked me so solemn.

"Yes, ma'am," I said, and I did. It meant Mrs. Rosen was in a gang!

Luz has a brother who has a tattoo on his arm that says "Latin King Love" with a date on it, and the boys who trade hood ornaments with Debergcrac also have tattoos, written in letters like King Arthur and his knights. And here was old Mrs. Rosen with a tattoo much plainer than theirs, but with some secret code clearly printed on her skin. Here was old Mrs. Rosen looking at me with eyes so big and unblinking, I could see the red of the inside of her lids. She looked as tired as I have ever seen her. Here was Mrs. Rosen, who had been in a gang!

"Did they maybe teach you a little bit in school?"

"Yes, ma'am," I said. The police lieutenant had

come to school and spoke to us very serious about wearing our shoelaces certain ways, about wearing an earring in one ear or a scarf in one pocket, what certain colors represent, and yes, about tattoos. I paid very good attention. "I know a lot about this," I told her.

"All of my family, they were all killed in the camps," she explained. "Aunts, uncles, cousins. My father, even, and two sisters. And my first love, though he died from being caught in the Resistance. He had eyes so warm and brown, like bread from the oven, little Paris. But did you think they looked once into the eyes that held his warmth, his soul? They shot him immediately. My mother is the only one besides me who made it out, and that was nothing short of a miracle. I only lived because I arrived in the camps so late."

What the heck sort of camps did they have in Paris, anyway? Here in America, I had never heard of anyone getting killed at the Youth Club camp. "Don't worry, Paris, it was a long time ago," said Mrs. Rosen in a watery voice.

Good, I thought. Even though I was very curious, I decided not to ask any more about it in case it wouldn't be polite. I didn't want Mrs. Rosen to feel too sad.

"Come with me," she insisted, and I followed her into her bedroom, where she opened a bureau drawer and pulled out an envelope, and in that envelope was a little yellow star with the word "JUIF" on it.

She fumbled with the stiff, tarnished pin. "I left Germany, but they followed, they spread, there was no escaping. I fought with the Resistance. All of us with eyes and ears could see what was coming, but when they came marching into Paris, I had no choice, you see, dear girl. They would shoot you in the street, like my first love, may he rest in peace." I nodded. I had heard the firing a few blocks over when there was a drive-by—yes, they shoot people in the streets who are on the wrong side.

"The neighbors there, they knew my family was going to be relocated, so they started fighting over my mother's belongings. This one wants the table, no, no, that one wants the table, the other one wants the kettle; it's still whistling on the stove and they can't wait until it cools. Believe me, Paris, these were not friends or neighbors, these were demons in house skirts. As soon as they heard the tromp of boots they said, 'Take her, take her.' "

"Take her where?"

"To hell, Paris. I hope you shouldn't know from hell." She knocked on wood.

"It's the place where the bad people go when they die," I said.

"No, sweetie." She patted my hand. "It's the place where bad people are in charge. You see, I didn't have to wait to die to see hell. I tried my best, I got papers and hiding places for more than I have fingers and toes, but what daughter does not in the end follow in her mother's footsteps, cursed though they may be? But now I'm talking too much. . . . You're too young. You shouldn't know. It will make you not right in the head if you know. Children shouldn't know. Children shouldn't know. . . ." She was upset, and seemed to not know if she was standing or sitting, coming or going. Where was Michael? The faint sound of a record playing whispered from behind the door.

"And here in my old age, hardly any of us left, I am torn between the desire to forget, and being left here to remember. And so I have kept it all these years," she said, softly touching the feathery frayed edges of the star, her fingertips over and over again

134

counting the six points, round and round. "I look at it, and all of the heartbreak comes flooding back. Does this pain make my loved ones live again? I should throw it away! Ptu, *ptu!* In the garbage it should go."

"No, don't do that." I pulled on her arm. "It must have some sentimental value if you kept it all these years."

"Oh, Paris, you are wise." Her hands trembled. "For all of these long decades, I felt like all the city of Paris owed me an apology for what was done to me and mine. And now, all that was sweet about it reappears to me in the form of you, a *ziskeit* who bears the same name, to remind me of what is good and to take from me the symbol of the lost years. Here, you will take it won't you, Paris? Some things are too much to remember all alone, and after I leave this earth, who will be left to remember?" With two hands, she handed me the star, and with two hands I accepted it. Here I was, Paris McCray, polite and protected, initiated into a gang of old, the last to remember its membership, like how they spray-paint on the rooftops R.I.P. *Pedro Never 2 Forget.* Mrs. Rosen was letting me into her most exclusive club. I bent my head like in church and said a prayer for those she had lost.

I didn't show the star to Michael because I didn't want him to be jealous that Mrs. Rosen gave me a special present, but I showed it to Django and Debergerac because they are streetwise and I thought they could tell me more about it. "That's not from any gang around here," they said.

"Are you sure?"

"Maybe it's a old lady gang," said Django.

"Yeah, yeah, you better recognize!" said Debergerac. "Wrinkles in the hizzouse!"

"Why does it say 'JUIF'?"

"I think that was her boyfriend's name. He was killed in a drive-by."

"Your piano teacher is so gangsta!" Django was impressed.

"Mrs. Rosen was a spy for her gang," I said. "In France. She got codes in invisible ink and she has a tattoo on her arm."

"No way," said Debergerac.

Django called Louis over. "Hey, that's from World War Two!" he said.

"So it's old? People don't wear them anymore?"

"Nope," he said. "You better take care of that. It might be valuable." Debergerac and Django looked at each other. "Not like that, you stupids. Valuable for history."

Django fingered the star greedily. I smacked his hand.

"That's pretty cool," said Debergerac. "Maybe you should bring the star to school and show it to your teacher. She might give you extra credit."

"Maybe I will," I said.

15

"WHAT'S THAT?" Sakiah asked when she saw the star pinned to my jacket the next morning.

"My piano teacher gave it to me," I explained. "She used to be in a gang, and this was the symbol of it. She wrote the name of her boyfriend in the middle. I think it's French for Jeff."

"We're not supposed to wear gang stuff to school," Cordelia was quick to remind me.

"She was the last one, she's all that's left to remember. The other gang doesn't exist anymore." I hoped I was right. "I told my piano teacher that I would remember her friends and family for her by wearing this star."

"That's nice," said Luz. "Maybe we should all make stars."

"Yeah, maybe we could remember soldiers," said Janine, "like how people wear ribbons."

This sounded like a good idea. More girls gathered around. A seventh grader almost tripped over her own feet when she saw me wearing the star, and she came marching over with her eyebrows bent all angry. "Hey, you! Take that off," she said.

"Get your own," I said. When I said these words, she looked suddenly like a torch was lit in her face, her eyelids turned the same orange color as her hair. She stomped off, like she was looking for a teacher, but on Wednesdays they are inside for a meeting.

"Well, I don't know why she is so mad," said Rashonda. "Maybe you should offer to make her one."

"Don't worry about it," snorted Angelina. "What one skinny white girl gone do?"

The bell rang, and we lined up to enter the building. Sahara joined the line and noticed the star.

"I think you should take it off," said Sahara, right away.

"Why?" I asked.

"I'm not sure," she said slowly. "I read a book once . . . There was a girl who wore one of those yellow stars. I remember it wasn't good to wear one of those."

Before she could say anything else, we passed Mrs. Eisenberg, the seventh-grade teacher. She looked at me sideways.

"Are you Anne Frank today?"

"No, I'm Paris McCray," I said, and kept walking.

"See? You should take it off." Sahara grabbed my arm. "Anne Frank was a girl who died from the Nazis."

"The who?" Was that the rival gang? I was starting to get nervous. Sahara reads a lot, and Sahara knows a lot, a whole lot more than Django and Debergerac about some things. So if Sahara said it wasn't a good idea, it probably wasn't. Why didn't I ask Louis more about it? I started fumbling with the pin, but it was stuck.

When I entered the classroom, Miss Pointy was not there yet, and Luz had already gotten out yellow paper from Miss Pointy's cabinet and was just finishing doing *kachoink-kachoink* on the mimeograph with a star design she had drawn. Cordelia was cutting them out, three at a time.

"Look, Look!" called Luz. "I remember how you do it, Paris."

"It goes so fast when you have the right machinery," said Cordelia.

Janine was using the stapler from Miss Pointy's desk to attach them to the tops of girls' shirts. Mariah had written the name "Deante" in the middle of her star. "He's in Iraq," she explained.

"I don't have any family in the military," said Rashonda. "Want me to put 'Deante' on mine, too?"

"Hey," said Raphael. "Are those just for girls? I have an uncle who died over there."

"They are for everybody," said Luz. "If you have someone to remember, you put their name on it, right, Paris?"

"I'm going to put my grandpa's name on it, then," said Leon. "He died, and I miss him."

"Do you want one?" Janine asked Tanaeja, who was sitting at her desk, unusual glum, looking at her lap and ripping paper into little pieces. Tanaeja pretended she didn't hear her, so Janine just clucked her tongue. "Well, you don't have to be like that!"

"Paris, you have the best ideas!" chirped Mariah.

"Sahara!" I pleaded.

"Stop it," Sahara did beseech to the class over the din of scraping chairs and laughter. I had a funny, spinny feeling as I watched everyone working on those yellow stars. "It doesn't mean what you think it means." Sahara's voice sounded helpless.

"What it mean, then?" asked Janine, but nobody could answer her. I thought of Mrs. Rosen and the red-faced girl on the playground, and had a quicksand feeling that I had made a terrible mistake. I felt my hands yanking at the star that was pinned to me.

Rachel tried to help. "This old pin is all rusted." Her arms dropped to her sides. "I'll get my scissors."

"No." I covered it with my hand. "We can't cut it. I promised Mrs. Rosen I would keep it."

"Well, Paris!" Sahara and Rachel looked at each other and huffed, like, *What do you want us to do, then?*

The second bell rang and in stepped Miss Pointy with all of her morning bounce. The class got right into their seats, hands folded, eager to show the good work they had done even before she had arrived. I think the word is *initiative*. Boris had even spelled out in neat letters on his star, "Miss Pointy." She seemed like her mind was trying to shake off the teachers' meeting and she was scrambling to get back into her groove. She opened her attendance book straight away and called out names double-time without looking up, and then, when she sang out, "Okay, anyone for paid lunch today?" she lifted her head.

When she saw us, all the color left her face, and all the smile did, too, and I swear, so did all the air and light in the room. She walked down the aisles, looking at each child wearing a yellow star and an exaggerated grin. "What is the meaning of this?" she asked in a soft voice, and it was hard to tell the way she felt. "I don't understand why you all have these yellow stars. Is this a special day I don't know about?"

"Nah! We are just being creative!" Sakiah called out brightly. I cringed. Sahara covered her face with her hands and shook her head.

"Yes, well, that's very good, I guess, but it's a *symbol*, children. Its not just a yellow star, it means something bigger than what it looks like. You can't just go writing people's names on these," she said. "People are liable to get offended." She came to Boris and ripped the star with her name on it off his shirt and crumpled it in one hand with a glinting of something like anger. Like a signal, the rest of the class ripped off their stars and stuffed them into their desks. All of them but me.

Miss Pointy looked at us as if she wasn't sure if she knew us, as if she couldn't find the right words to ask to make us hers again, until her eyes fell on me and my star that said JUIF, and even then she had to look twice to make sure she really recognized me, and this scared me more than anything I could name. Maybe Mrs. Rosen was right, there was a curse attached to this thing. Maybe whoever wears it is no longer the person they thought they were. Maybe when you wear this star, maybe you are not even a person at all to other people, maybe they look at you and all that they see is something low. Maybe the me that I had known had completely disappeared. I had never been in trouble at school before, not ever, and now, here was the biggest trouble I had ever been in, and for something I did not understand, just for being myself. Maybe that was enough of a mistake?

God help me! I prayed. She walked slowly up to me and reached down toward the star. I put my hand up to guard it. If it were destroyed, would there be anything left of me at all? Would Mrs. Rosen crumble into dust?

She moved my hand away and touched the star very gently. "Where did you get this?"

"My piano teacher give it to me." My voice was shaking, and I was trying not to cry.

"Paris McCray." She knelt way down on her knees to look me in my eyes. "Do you know what this star means?"

But before I could answer, the door opened, and there was Mrs. Eisenberg and the girl with the orange hair, pointing her finger at me.

Oooo oooo, first I was mad at Mrs. Rosen for giving it to me and then I was mad at Luz and Cordelia for printing up the stars on the mimeograph and then I was mad at Debergerac for telling me to bring it to school, but by the time I got to being mad at Sahara, I knew the one I should really be mad at was me. And maybe that carrottop girl. Why did she have to make such a big stink? Momma was called from work, from *work*! She came, and then there was a meeting where they figured out that I just didn't know. Know what? I wondered.

Mrs. Eisenberg said ignorance is not a defense, but I don't know what that means, except that then I had to do a report on World War II so I would know about the Nazis and the Jewish people and how those stars were used. Mom looked as uncomfortable as I did, but I guess after four boys you stay on the teacher's side as a matter of course. "If they are saying you did something to offend that girl, then you did. So you apologize, Paris, and do what you got to do to make it right."

"Where is the star?" asked the principal.

I looked to Miss Pointy, who had unpinned it from me. "Is it in your desk, Paris?" she asked.

"No, ma'am," I said. "You . . ."

"It will turn up," Miss Pointy interrupted.

Mrs. Eisenberg said I should have two days' in-school suspension off the record and in the library to work on my report and to read about that time period, and Miss Pointy looked worried. "She's only eleven," she said.

"Whatever she has to do to make amends, she will do it," promised Momma, who looked embarrassed. "We believe in the words of Martin Luther King at our house, and anything she did she didn't mean any harm by. Thank you for teaching her right from wrong where I could not."

The teachers seemed impressed by this.

I was not. In the hall, I was mad. "Momma, why you go apologize like that? You all begging them. What for? Calling you from work! Huh! I didn't do nothing wrong to Mrs. Eisenberg or that girl or none of them."

"Nothing, huh? You know about the Ku Klux Klan?"

I nodded. I had heard stories of the Klan, men wearing white sheets, burning crosses in the yards of black people down south in the middle of the night. Even though they didn't burn crosses on Clarendon Avenue in Chicago, I still had bad dreams about them when I was little.

"Well, I don't know much, but I know the Nazis, that's their Klan."

What was Momma saying? "I didn't burn a cross," I snarled.

"Didn't you hear that teacher? There comes a time when ignorance is no longer an excuse. Ignorance is the fire that burns the cross. Your ignorance." Momma whirled around. "People died, Paris.

People wore that star and died, the way people wore our skin and died."

"I didn't know, Momma!" I said helplessly.

"Now you *gotta* know," said Momma. "It's your time."

When I went to the library, Miss Espanoza gave me a pile of books. I opened the first one, and there was a picture of a little boy, his hands up in the air, surrounded by soldiers pointing their guns at him. He was wearing a yellow star.

16

WW II

I am sorry I am sorry I am sorry I did not
know, I would never ever have wore that
star if I knew. During WWII six million
Jewish people were killed by Nazi soldiers.
First they smashed the windows and then
many Jewish people had to hide and if the
Nazis caught them they

WW II

Anne Frank is an example of a person who
had to hide from the Nazis in a little room
for two years. She could not go outside and
she kept a diary and then they found her
and only her father

WW II

> The Holocaust was a very scary time in
> history when kids who were like you and
> I except they were Jewish but if you are
> Jewish they are still like you and

WWII

> In the camps conditions were very bad they
> shaved the women's heads and they lined
> them up and they
> And the old people
> And the sick people
> And the gay people
> And the gypsies
> And the artists
> And even the children
> The little children
> And furthermore for example
> For example
> 1.
> 2.
> 3.
> 6. million.

For weeks I read about those days, longer than

my in-school suspension, but I couldn't stop. I drank the pages like a poison that made me want to drink more poison, but still I couldn't write about it, it was too big. Once you know a little, oooo, this world, this glass-shattered black-and-white photographed world of hiding and gunshots, it comes into focus with nozzles spraying, with nooses and dogs and the whining of planes over the heads of the scattering, and the crowding of people into cattle cars. It wasn't enough, my world, my little world, just because I am a polite person, hey, I still notice the graffiti and the whistles from the gangs and the men sleeping in doorways. There was that drive-by this past summer with a stray bullet, didn't I notice that, wasn't that enough for a polite person to know about, Lord? But now, my eyes are drawn to the bigger world, to the newspaper headlines, to the buzzing of the radios and the flickering of screens, why didn't I see it all before? In Africa today . . . in China today . . . in Colombia . . . and here I am, one small person, I can't feed the hordes with bread and fish. I think about this world as Mrs. Rosen's arm rubs against me as she plays the piano, that arm that is evidence that it is true, they didn't make it up, it really did happen, those guns and camps and . . . Oh, God, your eye was not on the sparrow, was it? No big thing for them to starve a child. No big thing to separate a family. No big thing to take your mother's kettle while it was still whistling. . . . This world, this world, can this world be true? Will it come again? Is it happening right now, on the other side, where I can't see it with my own small eye? And what if my small eye is all there is to see it?

Oooo, but I do, I see it clearly, this reaping of helpless souls has gone on since the days the pastor speaks of from the pulpit, since the Romans, since David and that big old Goliath, since Moses and the Pharaoh, and in our time, too . . . and I am supposed to say Praise Him and be grateful just because it isn't me for now? What Lord would have let it all happen, what Lord would let it happen at all? It is this question that casts me from Eden. And still, all I know how to do is to ask Him to help me, help me, give it all back to me, all that I was before I knew. I want to wear those rose-colored glasses again, Lord!

And yet, even if the Horsemen of the Apocalypse are riding in, the school bell still rings. "How's your report coming?"

My report? Why was Miss Pointy asking about my report? With all that goes on in the world, she's asking about a *report*? I just shrugged.

"I notice you seem to be doing a lot of research. Do you need more time to work on it?" I nodded. "Okay, but please keep in mind, it has already been a couple of weeks. Mrs. Eisenberg's been asking. Just try to write something to show you have a sense of what that star means."

Oh, is *that* all?

"That reminds me." She pulled open the top drawer of her desk and took out a white envelope. Inside it was the star. "Here you go, Paris." I didn't make a move.

"That's okay, Miss Pointy. I don't want it," I said.

"You don't?"

"Nah. It's just a stupid little piece of cloth."

"Really?" Miss Pointy looked at me like she didn't believe me. "You think that?"

"Anyway, I don't know why my piano teacher gave it to me."

"She probably gave it to you because she thinks very highly of you," Miss Pointy explained in that sticky teacher way that's enough to drive a kid out of her skull. "But there is a lot of history attached. I understand if it's a bit much."

"Yeah, I'm too young," I agreed. "Children shouldn't know." But it's okay if I know, I thought. I may look the same in the mirror, but I am not the same because now I know what people can do. I guess in time I will turn inside out and the world will see the lines this knowing has cut in me. Inside, I am a little old lady like Mrs. Rosen. "History weighs heavy on the young mind, don't you think?" I suggested.

"Yes, I tend to agree." Miss Pointy looked at me fishy-like. "But maybe you were the only one she thought she could give it to."

"Maybe. But I just come for piano lessons." I think the word I felt was *desperate*.

"At any rate, I'll hold on to it. But just to let you know, it's not mine to keep, Paris. She gave it to you." I shrugged again. "You'll let me know when you want it back. And you'll let me know if you have any questions, won't you? Do you have any questions?"

I gave her a big smile. "No, ma'am," I said, and I didn't. I understood everything. There's people who act without reason, who tell themselves that they are *better than* and have a *right to*, so scary and bad that one mess of people can't even believe it enough to move, and a whole other mess of people are laughing and gathering 'round to watch the punches get thrown. That's how it starts, by letting bullies be bullies, right? You want me to ask a question? Try this: How long is long enough to suffer these fools? Before your hot angry defrosts your frozen fear? Before you just got to bear down and open up a can of down-home, hundred-proof I-think-the-word-is-*sanctified* nip-it-in-the-bud? 'Cause I saw how far it can go, how ugly it can get, in those books, on my brother's back, on Mrs. Rosen's arm, on the cross at the big church, and now it was all crystal clear: there's a time to be a polite person and a time for people to step up even at the risk of being as impolite as you have ever been.

Mrs. Rosen said, "Let's sing 'Oh, What a Beautiful Morning.'"

"Okay," said Michael. They sang it without me. Mrs. Rosen must have a very very bad memory. Or maybe she gave her memory to me when she gave me that star. Maybe she didn't remember anything anymore. Oooo, this makes me so angry. How am I supposed to keep coming here, singing these stupid songs when I know what I know? Why do I have to know, why do I have to be the one to know?

"Mrs. Rosen," I blurted, when the song was done. "I don't think I can come to piano lessons anymore."

"What?" said Mrs. Rosen.

"What?" said Michael.

I looked at these two people, these two soft people. In the forest where the hawk swoops down on the innocent, the little bird sings, This world, this world! But the bird still sings, doesn't it?

"Never mind," I said. "Keep singing."

"No," says Mrs. Rosen. "Tell me what's the matter."

"I have to write something for school," I sighed, "and it's too hard. It's too big an assignment."

"Not for my Paris," she says.

I wanted to tell her, The troops have marched in on your Paris, Mrs. Rosen.

"Come on, Paris," said Michael. "I want to be in good voice for the talent show."

"What are you talking about?"

"Hel-lo! 'All the Things You Are'? Eighth-grade talent show? You'll play for me, Paris, won't you?'"

"You want a prune, Paris?" asked Mrs. Rosen. "You look like maybe you could use a prune."

We walked along home and I did *stomp stomp stomp* on the sidewalk, to hell with the cracks, I stepped on every one of them and broke about a hundred mothers' backs, but guess what, big surprise, Michael was I think the word is *oblivious*. "You know what gets me, Michael?" I stopped walking. "You don't know nothing about the world."

"What are you talking about?" he asked.

"I'm talking about the world, Michael, *the world*! The world that has wars and death and starvation and bombs dropping and . . . and, Michael, you cannot get up and sing 'You are the promised kiss of springtime.' You just can't!"

"Why not?" asks Michael. "I bet Mose Allison would sing it."

"Well I don't know who Mose Allison is but let me tell you, he would get his butt kicked by Tanaeja, too," I point out. "OOoo, Michael, why? There are so many songs to sing. Why do you got to sing that one?"

"Because I love it," Michael said simply. "And when I get up and sing that song, there is going to be someone out there who will hear it, and it will make them brave enough to sing their own song and so on and so forth, and it will never end, Paris, do you see? I've got to sing my own song, I've *got* to sing it! It even says so in the Bible. 'Make a joyful noise.' And that, little sister, is what I know about the world. That, and that Mose Allison is a singer on one of Mrs. Rosen's records."

In his eyes I did see the fire of one who is ready to fight, that Michael was planning to use the promised kiss of springtime to kick the *derriere* of the world, if you'll pardon my French. I did see, too, that I have the bravest brother in the world.

And I did see 3. It was my turn to step up.

17

WHEN I CAME to school the next day, I no longer cared about being a polite person. It's just like Django and Debergerac say:

1. If you're likely to get in trouble for doing nothing you might as well get in trouble for doing something,
2. When a fight's coming, throw the first punch because then no matter what happens at least you'll know you got a good one in, and
3. Don't put your thumb inside your fist when you fight, because you can break it that way.

So when there were only a couple of minutes

until recess, I said to Tanaeja, "Guess what, I hope you got some nice ones in on my brother yesterday, because that's the last day you're going to get to do that."

"You and your brother," hissed Tanaeja. "You always flaunting him, walking with all your brothers around town. You think you all that."

What she is saying to me doesn't make sense, but I am wise now, I know things don't have to make sense, just that I have to take her down because This Cannot Continue. "Why do you beat on my brother?"

"What's it to you? He can defend hisself," she said. "Why he gotta be like that? It's wrong."

"Like what? He never did anything to anybody. He wouldn't even know your name if you weren't up in his face." I felt myself winding up, like one of Debergerac's toy cars that has a little coil that twists tighter and tighter before it spins so fast it smells like metal melting. "That's not right, Tanaeja, he can't hit you back because you're a girl."

"So is he," said Tanaeja. "He keep acting like that, he going to die."

I didn't even feel myself leave my seat. All I hear

is the screech of desks sliding and girls screaming. I feel my fingernails digging into the braids against her head. I feel her teeth wet against my cheek, trying to bite down. I feel people pulling us apart, but we're like Velcro, little barbs of a long, long anger hooked into each other. "Stop it, stop it!" Miss Pointy was shouting. Luz ran to the intercom button, chest heaving and big worried eyes, looking for Miss Pointy to tell her to buzz the office. But the recess bell had rung.

"You want to tell me what's going on?" Miss Pointy demanded, checking my cheek for cuts, checking Tanaeja's scalp for blood.

"Not really." Tanaeja crossed her arms.

"I'll tell you," said Darrell. "Tanaeja's been pushing Paris's brother around at recess."

"Be quiet," warned Tanaeja. "You-all better mind your business."

"Oh, yeah? What you gone do about it?" asked Darrell. "Bring it, Miss Dark and Lovely, just don't expect me to stand here and take it. I'm the man."

"Oh, don't start up, Darrell." Miss Pointy rolled her eyes.

"It's true! My brother has bruises all over his back, Miss Pointy," I told. I told!

"No he doesn't!" Tanaeja exploded.

"How would you know?" I felt my head reel around on my neck in a nasty way. "You think it's not gone come around, well I got news for you."

"I'll take you right here, Minnie Mouse." Tanaeja faced me.

"Ooo," said the class.

"What are you people still doing here?" Miss Pointy's voice rose. "Usually you can't get to recess fast enough. Trust me, nobody's bringing anything or taking anybody." The class gave us a wide berth as they filed out.

Miss Pointy looked back and forth between Tanaeja and me. "I'm very disappointed in you both. How do you expect there to be peace in the world if we can't even have peace in this classroom?"

"I don't expect it," I blurted.

For the second time, Miss Pointy looked at me and didn't seem to recognize who I was. It took her a beat or two before she could speak. "You think your mother needs this right now?" Miss Pointy asked Tanaeja.

"No, ma'am," said Tanaeja, rubbing her head with her forearm. I tried to hide my wondering about

162

what Momma would do if she were called in a second time, but Miss Pointy didn't seem to wonder if *my* mother needed this. Tanaeja started looking that same miserable way she uses in church. *You're kidding, right? Girl, you have got to be kidding.*

Then Miss Pointy told Tanaeja to go and cool off in the art teacher's room, and Tanaeja didn't need to be asked twice. Not fair, not fair!

"How come she gets to go?" I demanded, but then politeness set in. "I mean, you don't have to work on me first."

"I think I do." Miss Pointy pulled up a chair so I would sit right beside her. Then there was a long minute with just me and Miss Pointy. "This has been going on a while, huh? A lot going on," she said, finally.

My mouth was doing a crazy twitchy thing, turning down at the corners, and I could not look at her at all for what seemed like forever, but when I looked up, there she was, looking at me with the most concerned, sad expression I have ever seen. I burst out crying so hard that I put my head down on her desk. I could feel her patting me on the place where if I had wings, they would sprout.

"I'm trying to be brave," I finally said. I wanted her to say,

1. Poor Paris,
2. You *are* brave,
3. I know you are a polite person and that you would never behave this way if you weren't pushed.

Instead, she said, "So is Tanaeja."

"Who cares about Tanaeja?" I snorted

"I want to tell you something," said Miss Pointy, "and even though you are angry, I hope you will hear me. Sometimes people become our enemies not because they are so different, but because there is something in them that is so much the same, it hurts us to look at it."

"There's nothing about me that is the same as Tanaeja," I insisted.

"Maybe there's something about Tanaeja that is the same as you. Maybe you have something that she also has. Maybe you have something she is about to lose."

"What?" I asked.

Miss Pointy looked a little torn, like there was something she wanted to tell me but she couldn't. "Let's just say maybe there's something that you share that you don't know you share. That's not to say she can beat on your brother." Miss Pointy straightened. "That's going to stop."

"Miss Pointy, it can't seem like I was the one to stop it." It was so hard to explain. "He's got to stand up for himself."

"It's hard to stand up when someone is beating you down," said Miss Pointy. "Sometimes a person needs a little help. I'd even say *usually*, Paris. There's no shame in that."

"There isn't?" I asked, because

1. I felt ashamed so there must be some shame in it, and
2. Louis says some teachers were never kids and maybe she is one of them.

"But don't worry. It will look like I'm stopping it, because I'm the one who is. Got that?" I nodded. "Paris, I'll tell you something else. My best friend when I was a little girl started out as my enemy."

Luz is already my best friend, I thought, I don't need Goliath for a friend. But I just said, "Really?"

"It's true. She used to try to copy from my math test in class. I thought, She's sneaky, she's a cheat, she's going to get me in trouble, and I didn't want to have anything to do with her. In time, though, I saw that she wanted to do well in school, just like me, and I started helping her with her math before the test. She still calls me, Paris, we're still friends, twenty years later. But I haven't really learned my lesson. Even now, there are women I meet, and I'm still so quick to think, Oh, we don't have anything in common, but it always turns out we have *something* in common, or they have something about them that is interesting. Maybe not enough to be the best of friends, but it's enough to have a really good time together. But I wouldn't know that if I didn't push the doubts and prejudices aside so there is a little space in my heart for them."

The bell rang. Miss Pointy looked at the clock and sighed. "That space is where peace lives, Paris. That little spot in our hearts that has room for other people, that place where we try to find our common ground. Maybe it's all the peace we can expect, Paris. But let's try to keep expecting that much."

"Yes ma'am." I gulped. "I'll try."

I felt like I needed to wash my face. But I didn't want to go into the bathroom by myself. I still wasn't prepared to expect that much peace.

18

THEN ONE afternoon, everyone was working very quietly, because it was raining outside and something about thunder puts you in your place. There was a knock on the classroom door. The principal stuck his head in and called Miss Pointy into the hall. After a moment, Miss Pointy leaned back into the classroom.

"Tanaeja?" she called. "Tanaeja. Come here, dear."

"Ooo," said the class.

"Who, me?" said Tanaeja. "What did I do?"

"Nothing at all," said Miss Pointy. "Bring your things. Your mother is here, she's picking you up for early dismissal. Class, I need your best behavior for a moment." Her eyes flashed a warning.

"My mother is here?" Tanaeja gathered her things slowly and left. After a moment, there came a scream from the hallway that ran down my spine like a rip cord. "Not him." Tanaeja's voice came to us without her body. "No! No! No! God, no!" A tangle of faint grown-up voices calmed her, and faded, like echoes.

Janine stood up, and sat back down. We all looked at each other.

Miss Pointy came back into the classroom and stared out the window, her back to us.

"What happened?" Leon asked.

"Tanaeja's family has suffered a loss," Miss Pointy told the window. "She'll be gone for a few days. We all have to be extra nice to her when she comes back."

"We know," said Cordelia.

"I know you know," said Miss Pointy. "But I don't know what else to say."

"It's her brother, isn't it!" Kiarre pounded on her temples with her fists and sucked on her lower lip.

Janine put her head down on her desk and

started to cry. "He was sick a long time," she warbled from inside her arms.

Janine said a strong word but Miss Pointy didn't say anything about school language. She motioned to the washroom pass, and Janine went.

I didn't know she had a brother. I didn't know she had a brother that was sick. I didn't know. I thought about this girl in her purple dress, crying in the fifth pew of the church, and my ugly thoughts. *Who she think she is. Who she fooling. Guess even the Devil can dress up on Sundays.* I felt numb all over.

We collected money for flowers.

19

FOR LOUIS's eighteenth birthday Momma and Daddy offered to treat us all to a night at a restaurant, but instead Louis asked if we could have takeout from Jake's Chicken, because that is his favorite. He also told us he was going to bring a special guest, and that he was going to give us all a present for his birthday. We were kind of excited; none of us had gotten a present on someone else's birthday, unless you count goody bags. I was surprised when the special guest he went to pick up turned out to be Luz's big sister, Eva, looking very nice in her short skirt and big pink T-shirt and matching headband. Soon as she walked in the room, though, Momma started acting like an alley cat, skirting around the far side of the room from this girl, all the while her eyes on her. I bet the hair on her back was standing up.

At dinner, everyone could feel the tension. Daddy tried to break it. "What's this?" Daddy laughed. "It's so quiet at the table. We must all be hungry!"

Django and Debergerac kind of chuckled like idiots at the nonjoke. Louis and Eva exchanged glances, and Momma chewed her chicken with arrows shooting out of her eyes.

Then Louis wiped the grease off his hands with a paper napkin and stood up. "Mom," he said, "Dad."

"Louis, Louis, Louis, you don't need to say a word." Momma threw her chicken down, looked at my father, and howled, "He got her pregnant!"

My father stopped chewing and looked from Louis to Momma. "What?" he said, with his mouth full.

"I could smell it the minute she walked into the room. A mother knows. You got that?" She pointed at Eva. "No use acting all quiet and shy, little girl. I got your number, including your area code, and there ain't nothing about you that I need to know that I don't already know."

"Is this true, son?" asked my Daddy.

"Yes, sir," said Louis. Both he and Eva were looking at their laps.

Momma lowered herself down to her chair from her state of levitation, and we sat quietly for a minute, bringing new meaning to the term *pregnant pause*. We were swirling french fries around in the ketchup, like nothing had happened at all, until Daddy said, "Well, at least he can play the guitar."

"Play the guitar!" Momma railed. "Oh, sister, wait until you figure out what you've signed on for!" She laughed a hard laugh that sounded like a chicken bone was stuck in her throat.

"Now that is uncalled for." My father's mouth got crumply.

"Uncalled for, nothing! He's supposed to do better, you all are supposed to do better. What did I tell you when he got that car? I told you, 'Nuh-uh, have him bring it back and get something with bucket seats. No good ever came out of an Impala.' That's what I said, does anyone recall? Nobody listens to a thing I say in this house, let me tell you what!" She sat back down on her chair, hard.

"If it's a girl, you gone name her Lala?" asked Debergerac.

Ooooo, it is a girl, I thought. I just know it.

"What about California, Louis? What about school? Do you know what happens to a dream deferred?" asked Momma. "It explodes, Louis. It explodes!"

"Then why are you the one exploding, Momma?" asked Louis. "Those were my dreams, not yours. And I don't mind deferring them, neither. I got a different dream on the way." I never noticed before how deep Louis's voice had become.

"Her parents kicked her out the house because they're not married," Django informed us, by way of changing the subject. Louis did a silent murder face, and Django did a what-did-I-do face.

"Well, that's brilliant," said my mother. Eva looked like she wanted to say something, but Louis patted her hand. "So I suppose you think you're staying here."

"Please, Momma," said Louis. "Just till I save up

enough to rent an apartment. I can do it. I did it for the car."

"He did it *in* the car," whispered Django. The table jumped as someone kicked him.

"Should have made him take the bus," grumbled Momma, and then she waved her finger around the table and shouted, "The rest of y'all are taking the bus!"

"It will be a pretty baby, Momma," I said quietly.

"You shut up," she snapped. "And where that pretty baby gone sleep? In the bathtub?" I wanted to tell Momma what Mrs. Rosen told me about babies sleeping in open dresser drawers when she first came to America, but I guessed since she told me to shut up like an impolite person, I wouldn't, so there.

"How far along are you?" Momma demanded.

"Four months." You could barely hear her.

"Four months!"

"We were waiting until I turned eighteen to tell you," Louis explained.

"Why wait? It takes more than candles on a birthday cake to make a man," said Momma.

"That's enough!" Daddy's voice had bang to it like his bass drum. "Now, we are not the first family

174

in the history of the world that this has happened to," Daddy said reasonably, talking like his drumsticks with brushes at the end, *husha-husha-husha*. "We will work it out. Welcome to the family, Eva."

"You made me a grandma at forty," said Momma. "Louis, I'll never forgive you."

I did not know Momma could be such a bad sport.

That night, Michael was so excited that he couldn't even lie down, so he snuck into my room. He was pacing back and forth in his pajama bottoms that came up about three inches over his ankles. "I'm going to get to use the ricer!" he was saying. "I never get to use the ricer. I'll put bananas and sweet potatoes through. Do babies like peas, or are they like everyone else? I wonder if there are cookbooks for baby food?"

I had my own questions running through my mind. "Does this make me and Luz sisters?" I wondered aloud.

"Oh, man." Michael broke into song, " 'There is a rose in Spanish Harlem!' You know what, Paris? I think this is going to be the best time our family has ever had. 'A rose in black and Spanish Harlem!'" He cha-cha'ed in front of my window, the shape of him surrounded by the glow of streetlights, and the high thumbnail moon resting on his head like a crown. Through the crack in the door to Louis and Michael's room, I could see Eva watching him, too, pale and quiet like the moon, Louis's strong arm folded around her body, her half-smile peeking out from under the blanket.

20

A WEEK PASSED, and Tanaeja returned to school. She looked stiff and ashy and tired, and her mouth looked sewed on, like a doll's.

"Sorry about your brother," said Leon. "Even if you knew it was coming, it's got to be hard."

Ameer poked Leon for saying anything. "Man!" Leon cringed, and looked embarrassed.

The thread of Tanaeja's mouth look pulled and crimped, as if she were swallowing a pill. "No, Ameer, it's all right. Thanks, Leon," she choked.

Miss Pointy smiled gently at Tanaeja, and started the day's lessons. She didn't call on Tanaeja much, and when she did, Tanaeja didn't answer. Janine sent me notes to pass to her, but when they arrived, Tanaeja just put them in her desk.

That afternoon, Darrell announced, "I want to show my movie."

"Darrell, I have lesson plans," said Miss Pointy.

"Be that way." Darrell pouted. "Don't let me show a one-minute movie."

"Wouldn't you rather wait and have a premiere? I don't even have popcorn," Miss Pointy said.

Darrell shook his head. "Now. It's just one minute long."

"I'd kind of like to see it first." Miss Pointy looked suspicious.

"Dang, woman, why you give me a camera and then don't let me show a one-minute movie? Nothing the class hasn't seen. I just had a machine in my face." He glared at Rashonda, who glared back.

Miss Pointy looked like she was deciding what would take longer: arguing with Darrell or letting him have his way. Finally, she pulled a TV/VCR out of the corner and hooked up the camera. "You have one minute, Darrell." She set an egg timer.

"*Before: A Darrell Sikes Joint,*" he announced.

Pan of classroom, one by one. We are working. Thunder rumbles. There is a knock at the door. The principal sticks his head in and says, "Miss Pointy, may I see you out in the hall? Now?"

Miss Pointy stood up like she sat on a tack. "Darrell Sikes! We are turning this off right now!"

"It's over anyway," Darrell gloated. The egg timer sounded. The tape rewound itself.

"Tanaeja, I'm so, so sorry," Miss Pointy apologized, red-faced, like she had done something wrong. "I had no idea. I would never have . . . that was irresponsible of me . . ."

But we weren't mad at her. How could she know Darrell would do something so terrible, tape someone about to learn her brother . . . and then show it? Was he a monster? Was he an actual *monster*? Tanaeja just stared at the black screen, without blinking, her mouth unhinged.

"Darrell, that's low," said Dominique. "Something's wrong with you."

"Show it again," said Tanaeja.

"What?"

"She said, 'Show it again.'" Darrell puffed up like

a rooster. Miss Pointy looked like she didn't know what to do. The screen filled again. Again, the camera's eye—was it really Darrell who was looking at us?—moved from student to student. It passed over Tanaeja, working, like the rest of us, not knowing what was moving down the hall, toward her. There was a shot of us as a whole class, working. It showed the strange shadows the rain made against our faces, as though we were made of . . . of weeping, of a sadness present in the room, but hidden to us.

The knock came, a beat, and, "Tanaeja?" Closeup. "Tanaeja. Come here, dear."

Tanaeja. Come here, dear.

Tanaeja. Come here.

"Who, me?" Tanaeja looking up, surprised. The screen went black.

We sat silently for a moment. "That's a very sad movie, Darrell," Miss Pointy determined.

Tanaeja had lines of tears running down her face, down her neck, but she was smiling. "No, no, it's not," said Tanaeja. "You don't understand. It's not about the saddest day of my life. It's about the happiest moment of my life. The moment before . . ." She choked, and started crying hard.

Miss Pointy reached for a tissue herself, and then handed the box to Tanaeja. "Janine," she said. Janine got up and started to take Tanaeja to the girls' room, I guess.

"Wait," said Darrell. He hit the eject button and handed Tanaeja the tape. "You can have it." She nodded, and they left.

We didn't say anything for a moment. There was something in my throat, I couldn't gulp it down. Kids were turned sideways at their desks, looking at their shoes, wiping their noses on their sleeves. Tanaeja had taken the box of tissues.

"How did you know that was the right thing to do?" asked Kiarre. "I didn't know the right thing to do."

"How you think I know?" Darrell sounded disgusted.

This bad, bad boy's eye was on the sparrow, I thought. Right here in this room. He was his sister's keeper. And where was I?

"Good joint, Darrell." Rashonda sniffed and wiped her eyes, and smiled his way.

Darrell ignored her. "I need a new tape," he demanded, and sat down.

21

WALKING HOME, I told Michael that Tanaeja was back. He sighed. "I had better call her," he said.

"What are you talking about?" I hissed. "Her brother just died. She's going to be madder than ever at you."

His eyes went wide. "What for?"

"Don't you get it?" I said. "She's jealous. Something about you must have been like her brother. She knew he was dying and she was mad and she took it out on you." I thought about the things she said. *Why he got to be like that? Why he got to be so soft?*

You keep flaunting him, you think you all that. He keep acting like that, he going to die. I wondered, did her brother make chocolate mousse, sing along with records, come in her room at night and talk to her until she fell asleep? I shivered at the thought of the empty place he must have left.

"Well, there's nothing more to take out."

"Ha!" I laughed. "You don't think she's mad that he's dead?"

Michael turned and looked at me hard. "You still don't like her, do you?" he asked.

"Do *you*?"

"I just know what she's done. And what's happened to her. I don't know her," said Michael.

"I know she's a bully who beats on my brother."

He sighed. "Give me her number. I know you got it on those Extreme Readers forms you passed out."

"No, Michael."

"Fine," he said. "Come on, I know where she lives." He grabbed my arm so tight, it hurt. He started pulling me along with him.

"No!"

"Yes, Paris! Why you got to be so hard?"

"Why you got to be so soft?" I whirled around and shook him off. "She was probably right about you all along. Nobody else would take it like you. . . . The way you fight, like you're shooing a fly. Are you a freak, or what?" Michael's eyes shifted, looking to see if anyone on the sidewalk might have heard. Right away, I felt bad. Momma says words are like toothpaste. Whatever you squeeze out, you're going to have a hard time getting it back in the tube, and she's right. "You're not a freak, Michael, I take it back, you know I don't think that. I'm sorry. That's not what I meant. I'm just tired, Michael. Why do I have to step up for you every time? It's done me in. Can't you see that?"

"I never asked for you to step up for me." His cheeks flushed, and muscles rippled in his jaw.

"Well, you won't do it for yourself."

"Do what? Give her a black eye? A bloody nose?"

"Yes!" I shouted.

"And be sent to the principal's office? Have Momma and Daddy lose time from work? Get suspended? Have guys in my class whale on me for bullying a fifth grader?"

"All right, all right," I said.

"More fights? Not get considered for the high school arts program? Not graduate with my class? Have her come back with a knife? A gun? Make a girl cry? Huh? Yes to that, too?" said Michael, his voice rising. My brother never talks to me like this. "Don't you think I've thought about it, Paris? I am so tired of this! Don't hold my grudges for me! You are so spoiled! Everybody likes you, Paris, you've got a ton of friends, right? You're the baby, you're the club president, you're the boss, you're a star. You can do no wrong." He stopped walking altogether. "Well, not everybody likes me, and maybe that's the way it's going to be, but that doesn't mean they can tell me who to like. Do you understand?"

My eyes were welling up. "I'm sorry, Michael."

"No, I'm sorry for you." He flung my arm aside. "There's a girl in your class whose brother is dead. Are you going to express your condolences or not? Because I am."

I didn't know what to say.

"And anyway." He started walking again. "A deal's a deal."

"What are you talking about?"

He paused a little bit, like he was deciding

whether or not to tell me. "Remember when you were little, and I swung you around and you banged your head on the corner of the fireplace and it bled all over and Momma . . . It looked like I killed you, Paris, I really thought I had killed you. I felt terrible. I prayed to God. I said, 'God, if you let my sister live, I will live a peaceful life. I will be gentle, I will never roughhouse again. I will never act in such a way that will cause another to bleed.' And then you lived, and Momma brought you home." He smiled a satisfied smile, like he had saved my life. "And that's when I chose my instrument."

"What instrument?"

"Me!" He raised his eyes heavenward. "I am an instrument of Thy peace."

"Well, you're a real virtuoso," I had to admit.

"Thank you." He laughed.

"But, Michael, you shouldn't hang on to that silly little accident. I'm fine, see? It happened a long time ago. God doesn't expect you to keep that promise."

"He expects me to *try*," he explained. "God expects you to *try* to keep your promises. And I promised to try to be good, so I'm going to try."

"You still roughhouse with Louis," I pointed out.

"Big farting brothers don't count," he said matter-of-factly.

Later, I sat on my bed and tried do my homework, but my head was filled with imagining God whispering to every little baby, "Try to be good, just *try*," before he sends them down the heaven chute to Earth. Then when you get back up to the gate, He probably asks, "Did you *try*?"

It is a fair question.

I got Tanacja's Extreme Reader form from the shoe box under my bed. It took me a long time before I could dial without making a face like someone was biting my foot. Michael came in and watched me with his arms crossed. When I finally dialed, I hung up. It was Michael's turn to roll his eyes.

Less than five minutes later, the phone rang.

"Hello?"

"Is this Paris?"

"Yes. Who is calling, please?"

"What you mean? This is Tanaeja. You just called my house."

"H-how did you know I called?" I stammered.

"Caller ID. What you want?" I took so long to answer that she said "Hello" again, to check if I was still there.

"I forgot," I answered, feeble-like.

Tanaeja grunted. "Well, don't be calling here after dinner. My momma needs to keep the phone line open."

"All right," I said. "Sorry."

I felt so stupid. Why did I say sorry? *She* should say sorry. "Ask her if she wants to come over," prompted Michael.

"Wait! My brother wants to talk to you," I said, and then we had a silent-film fight over the phone until he finally took it.

"This is Michael. You know, Paris's brother?" There was a pause. "Yes, that one, unfortunately, ha-ha!" I could see his Adam's apple move up and down as he swallowed. "I was wondering if you might want to come over and make brownies?"

I guess she answered. When Michael handed the phone back to me, no one was on the line. I I banged the receiver down five times.

"Well, I feel like a real grown-up," he said.

"Yeah, Martin Luther King would be proud," I sneered.

"You think so?" His eyes sparkled.

I sighed. "What did she say?"

"She said she would come if she could bring a friend."

"That's because she's scared we're going to jump her. She should be."

"Maybe you should keep hood ornaments under your bed if you so bad." Michael moved his head around his shoulders to make fun of my girl-attitude. "Well, if she's bringing a friend, I'm calling Frederick."

"Frederick can't do anything," I said, disgusted.

"He can bake brownies!" Michael reminded me.

There she was in my kitchen, in a too-big apron, standing between Frederick and Michael, stirring a bowlful of batter. The counter was covered in flour and cocoa. Frederick had chocolate goop smeared on the corner of his glasses. Debergerac and Django were sitting at the table. I made them stay in case she started up. But from what I could tell, they were on straight-up bowl-licking duty. Janine had a chair squeezed in between them, trying to frost and put sprinkles on a finished tray while her shoulders were all pulled in from lack of room. I just sat there with them, not believing my enemy was in my kitchen.

"We'll make three batches," Michael ordered. "Don't stir it too much; they'll be like cake then. Add more oil, so they're moist. I'm sorry about your brother, Tanaeja. But don't beat me up anymore, okay? I don't like it." My brothers stopped moving, their batter-covered fingers poised in their mouths.

"Okay," she almost whispered.

"You remind me of Tanaeja's brother," said Janine, bright and cheerful. "He was a lot older, like a young grown-up. But he was tall like you and dark, and something else about you reminds me of him."

"Sweet?" said Django, real innocent.

"Well, yeah," said Janine. "Kind of."

"Don't talk about my brother," Tanaeja said in a threatening way, but Janine wasn't fazed.

"Why not?" She sucked some frosting noisily off her finger. "Don't you want to remember him?

I want to remember him. He was nice."

Tanaeja started crying. Michael didn't blink. "Enough salt in the brownie batter," he said. He put his arm around her and gave her a squeeze.

22

I DECIDED TO make a special edition of the
Extreme Readers Extra.

Hello, it is me Paris McCray and I am
writing to say I am so sorry for the
confusion about the yellow star. I could
use up this whole paper saying sorry,
because that is how sorry I am. You see I
was ignorant about what the yellow star
meant and I know I was not the only one. So
the best thing I can think of to do is to
tell you what I know about it. Even if
you are Black or speak Spanish so what

this is important like civil rights.

We were not completely wrong when we made our own stars. Yes they are about remembering people, but they are for remembering people who lived and died during the terrible time of World War Two, spelled WWII for short. What time is that you may ask. So here is information. German soldiers called Nazis who followed a leader named Hilter killed millions of Jewish people in the 1930s and 1940s. The Nazis made all the Jewish people wear this star on their clothes so they could tell who to kill. Children and moms and dads and grandparents and teachers were all included. Also people who weren't Jewish, just different than the kind of people that Hitler liked. This killing was called the Holocaust. Hitler wanted people to be all the same. He didn't know that we need all kinds of people to make a world.

You may ask why didn't the Jewish people just fight back. Well, some did but they were caught off guard because they were trying to be good, they weren't trying to start a fight. They couldn't believe people would be that unusual bad. So they got beat on for a long time. Even though the Nazis were hateful like the Klan, there were so many of them that they didn't hide their faces. Instead, many Jewish people had to hide in order to survive. Others had to live in ghettos, but different from ghettos in Chicago, these had walls around them so people couldn't get out. Some were sent to camps, but nothing like summer camps, people died in these camps. Some of the Jewish people tried to be proud of the star, because it was part of who they were.

If you would like to see a real star from WWII, for example, it is on display in the school library. Thank you to Mrs. Rosen for the loan of this valuable artifact. Also thank you to Miss Espanoza for helping me to make this list of books that will help us to know and to remember so a Holocaust does not happen again, or if it starts to,

maybe we will recognize and try to stop it
before it gets too bad. Be careful when you
read these books, though, because you might
feel too sad and almost sick like you can't
do anything, or like you can't feel anymore
and it doesn't matter what you do. You can't
really escape it, just watch TV and you'll
see. But try not to feel so sad. That is not
our job. I think our job is to 1. Be doubly
happy to make up for all those children
who didn't get to live and be happy, 2. Be
grateful for family, and 3. Remember how
bad people can be as a reminder of how
good we have to try to be. Just try. Really,
really try. P.S. It's hard.

Miss Pointy was so glad, she hugged me when
she read what I wrote. I was excited to show it to
Mrs. Rosen. I wanted to tell her, too, how Mrs.
Pointy was going to help us study about World War
II in class, so we could learn about it all together and
she could do a better job answering questions. She
thought maybe Mrs. Rosen could come and visit the
class. I was going to tell Mrs. Rosen that, and the

news about Louis and Eva, but I thought I would wait until after Michael's performance.

I didn't wait, though, to tell Mrs. Rosen about how Michael made peace with Tanaeja. "What a mensch," she said. "A real person, your brother is. And that Tallulah, sounds like she turned out to be not such a monster after all." She was sitting on the sofa in the living room, eating a cheese omelet, while I practiced a hard song called "After You've Gone."

"It's Tanaeja, Mrs. Rosen," I said. "And I'll bet she hits him again."

"Since when are you a gambling woman?" She tried to dismiss my big feelings with a wave of her magic fork.

"Well, why wouldn't she?"

"I guess she might," said Mrs. Rosen. "But she might not. Are you jealous?"

"Of what?"

"Of your brother baking brownies with her in the kitchen, maybe?" I didn't answer her. "If you want my personal opinion, you're going to have to suck it up. A boy who can bake brownies is going to be very popular. Your brother is going to be loved by many people, Paris. But do you know who he will always love? The one who can play the music to accompany his song."

I stopped playing. "You're coming to the assembly, aren't you? There's not enough room in the car, so Louis is going to drop off my family and then he'll be back for you. He'll be by for you at a quarter to one. Can you be ready at a quarter to one?"

"Why do you say the time twice? What do you take me for, an old person? I'll be waiting downstairs with bells on," said Mrs. Rosen. "Unless this cheese omelet catches up with me, I wouldn't miss it for the world."

I played really well for Mrs. Rosen that afternoon. I sang "I'm a little jazz bird." She liked that.

Michael came out of the record room, and we practiced for an extra hour. "Maybe I'll do 'When You Wish Upon a Star,'" he said.

"Yeah, do that one," I begged.

"Maybe for an encore after 'All the Things You Are.'" He grinned wickedly.

"Don't forget the hat," said Mrs. Rosen as we were leaving. "See, I remember better than you."

23

THERE IS SOMETHING about having to perform in front of a lot of people that makes a person have to pee. For example, when I walked into that cafetorium full of scraping chairs and an elevated stage setup and a room full of hooting big kids, I turned around and headed straight for the girls' room, almost running through the swinging doors, but then I pulled up real short.

There was Tanaeja.

We stared at each other.

"Hi," she said.

"I got to use the bathroom," I said and went into a stall, but the door's lock was broken so I just had to hold the door closed. There is something about having to pee when someone else is in the girls' room that makes it hard to perform. I was waiting to hear the hinges swing so I would know Tanaeja had gone. But I could only wait so long.

"I never had any beef with you," she said on the other side of the door.

Well, I had a beef with you, I thought. Then I sighed. I could not stay in the stall forever.

I came out and said, "I'm sorry about your brother." Which I was. "But you know, just because something bad happens to you, you don't get to do people like that."

"You talking to me, or to yourself? All high and mighty," she grumbled.

I caught my reflection in the silver hand-towel dispenser, my pigtails tied in neat ribbons for the performance. Don't get in another fight, I told myself. You'll get all messed up.

"But I am sorry, like I said. I wouldn't wish losing a brother on anyone." *Even you,* I added inside my head. I started washing my hands. She was just standing there, behind me. Why didn't she hurry on back to class?

"Anyway, you know that girl? That wasn't really me. I mean, not the *real* me."

"No?" How many *me*'s she got? I wondered. I also wondered how long I could wash my hands without this rancid pink soap peeling off my skin.

"Paris, look, I said I was sorry. I won't bother your brother again. We had a fine old time at your place. Michael is a good cook."

"There's a lot of good about him," I said.

"Yeah, I know," she said, I think the word is *defeated*, and I had a feeling she was thinking about her brother as much as mine. "And I really did read those books," she tried to add, all bright and sunshiny. I was so mixed up by her trying to be this new "real" her that it took me a second to know what she was talking about. "So I was hoping we could be friends. Not just him and me. Me and you, too."

I didn't think so, I really didn't think so, but I thought about what Miss Pointy said. *It always turns out we have something in common. Maybe not enough to be the best of friends, but enough to have a really good time together.* "I don't know, Tanaeja," I said.

"See you in church?" she asked.

Purple dress, fifth row. "See you in church," I said.

The cafetorium was louder than before, if that could be possible. I slid into the front row because the performers had to be close up. Michael was beside me, wearing the hat with the feather in it and holding his hands between his knees. "What took you so long?" he asked, which I think is a rhetorical question.

I had the sheet music on my lap, and practiced my finger movements on an invisible piano. "Sing slow," I told Michael. "Take your time. Listen to make sure I'm caught up, okay?"

Michael didn't seem to hear me. "Is Daddy here?"

I half-stood and tried to make him out in a sea of heads. "I don't know, Michael. I think they are sitting too far back."

"He never missed Louis's football games, you know."

"Those were on Saturday afternoons, Michael, that's why, and you know it. And anyway, he'll be here."

"What if he got called in to the studio?"

"He's not going to the studio," I said. "Everything's going to be fine. You'll be fine."

"I've got a weak voice," he choked.

"You got a cabaret voice," I said. "Mrs. Rosen said so that time, remember?"

"He's going to hate it," he growled. "He's going to be 'shamed of me."

Why was Michael all fixating on Daddy? "Why do you say that? He's heard you sing at home."

"I want Daddy to see me do good," he said. "Out here, in the world. Like Louis does."

The principal stepped up to the microphone and tapped. We were going to begin.

Michael looked at me and just smiled, if you could call that rumpled nauseous lip thing he was doing a smile. He looked like he was going to be sick. He started to rock back and forth. "Daddy is going to love it," I assured him. "And Momma and Mrs. Rosen. And Louis and Eva. And Frederick."

"Shhhh!" Someone shushed us from behind.

"And Mose Allison. And Bill Evans. And Josephine Baker. And Dr. King and Ella Fitzgerald and Cole Porter and Jerome Kern, wherever they are, they're all going to love it. And someone whose name you don't even know," I whispered. "There is going to be someone out there who will hear it and it will be make them brave enough to sing their own song and so on and so forth, and it will never end, do you see?" He still had his hands between his knees and was rocking, but he was smiling for real now. "And know who else is going to love it? Me, Michael. I'm going to love every minute of it. So you get up there and make your joyful noise. Don't you be afraid to be happy. That's your star quality." He let out a watery laugh.

"Shhh!" someone said again.

I turned around. "Shhhh yourself!"

I didn't know why someone was shushing us anyhow, it was the same old thing, girls doing stupid cheerleader routines they learned from their older sisters, and boys rapping so close to the microphone that you couldn't make out the words, the white kid who can play "The Star-Spangled Banner" on violin, and a girl singing "I Believe I Can Fly" an octave out of her range, but it's okay because who cares, you could hardly hear her over the tape anyway. I wondered what Mrs. Rosen thought of the girl's belly button showing. I craned my neck, but couldn't see more than two rows behind.

Then the principal introduced us and I squeezed Michael's hand so hard I almost crushed it. It was an upright piano, and I couldn't see over it to see Michael, I could only see a sliver of the audience. I looked over the side and saw him give me a thumbs-up. So I began to play. I heard the usual big bad boys jeering and whooping, but they were quickly silenced. And then we were in our groove.

Michael was singing slowly. When I stopped, he stopped. He was listening to me! I tried to pretend like we were in Mrs. Rosen's apartment, in our own little world. Then I started to enjoy myself. It *is* our own little world, I thought. It's anything we make it to be.

I wouldn't say the applause was thunderous, more like I think the word is *perplexed*, but when we were done, the principal took the microphone and thanked everyone for coming and told everyone to stay in their seats until their rooms were called for dismissal. My family rushed up, and Daddy put Michael in a headlock and rubbed his fist into his head. "I knew he'd be the one!" he almost shouted to no one in particular. "I've got to take him to open mike. You'll play the Green Mill, son! Did you all see that? That was class, right there. Class and guts. I knew if you hung around that Mrs. Rosen, it would all rub off. You see that, son? Your old man had plans for you." Daddy's chest was puffing out so much, it looked near bigger than Momma's.

Momma was hugging me and kissing the top of my head. "Where is the famous Mrs. Rosen?"

Yes, where was she? I looked at the students filtering through the rows, but she was nowhere to be seen. I looked to the back double doors. There was Louis, just standing against the wall beside the door, his face ashen and frowning. Even from far away, I looked at him, and I knew.

I broke away from my mother and ran behind the upright piano. I scrunched up my eyes as hard as they could go and tried not to breathe. I tried to make the world turn in the other direction. Trying to bring back the moment before I knew.

24

MOMMA MADE US all dress up to go to the lawyer's office. The little bald man looked even smaller beneath the tall wall of bookshelves. He seemed vaguely surprised to see us. He pulled out a long, brown cardboard box from behind his desk. "Which one of you is Michael?" he asked.

Michael pulled open the flaps. "The records!" he shouted like it was Christmas morning. Then he pulled out from the front of the box a worn gray book held together with rubber bands. "The Jerome Kern songbook." He held it to his chest with both arms and sighed. "She left me everything."

"Not quite everything," said the lawyer. "Five thousand dollars to be set aside in a trust for Paris McCray, to be given to her on the occasion of her twenty-first birthday so that she may visit Paris, France."

I felt, I think the word is . . . I don't know. There is no word for it. My mother bit down on her lower lip and tears fell from her eyes. My father rubbed the back of her head, and Eva and my brothers hummed.

"It's like you won a game-show prize!" said Debergerac.

"Are you the custodian of the trust?" Daddy asked the lawyer.

"Mrs. Rosen named you, her parents, the custodians of the trust."

"What's a trust?" I asked.

"It's a special account that is being held in your name until you are older," the lawyer explained.

"Does that mean that if I want to take it out of the trust, my parents can decide if I may?"

"Yes," said the lawyer. "Your parents can dissolve the trust. But Mrs. Rosen was very specific in her wishes for this trust, Paris."

"You'll go to France, honey," said Momma. "Just

like I always wanted to." She looked at the lawyer. "Of course, we will maintain the trust."

I took a deep breath. "I wish to dissolve the trust," I said firmly. "I wish to give the money to Louis so he can get his own apartment with Eva and the baby."

My family looked at each other, worried that I had gone crazy. I could see my parents struggling with the suggestion.

"The apartment isn't big enough for two more," I reminded them. "We all know it."

I could see Louis squirm. Louis, who worked at the ballpark all summer. Louis, who had his own car and was Daddy's Big Help. I thought of the day so long ago that I held up three fives in front of Mrs. Rosen. *I would do it for free, but I don't want you should be ashamed.* "If you wanted to, you could name the baby Hannah," I told Louis. "After Mrs. Rosen's mother."

"Hannah. Hannah." Daddy played it in the air for all to hear.

"Better than Lala, anyway," Django whispered to Debergerac.

Louis was chewing away on his lower lip,

but Eva put her hand on his shoulder.

"Or maybe," suggested Eva, "if it is a girl, we could name her Rosa, after Mrs. Rosen."

"Like a Rosen in black and Spanish Harlem!" Michael crowed.

"Is it a deal?" I asked. Louis looked at my parents, unsure how to answer.

"But, Paris," said my mother, "that's not what Mrs. Rosen wanted. Mrs. Rosen wanted you to see the city you were named after. Mrs. Rosen wanted you to go to Paris."

I thought about Mrs. Rosen, my jazz bird, her hands flying across the keys. I thought about matzoh ball soup and chopped-liver sandwiches. I thought about a yellow star and a tattooed arm. I thought about a living-room cancan and ginger-ale champagne and my brother's voice floating. I thought about a little girl in a world of war listening to a bird singing in the woods like it doesn't even notice what's going on. I thought about a man at a pulpit preaching things I only half understand, things I want to understand so, so much, things that I will only begin to understand if Louis takes this money. I thought about rose-colored glasses and a walk to Paris that lasted seven blocks. Seven blocks of walking on our own, in the right direction.

I put on my rose-colored glasses once more, though nobody could see them. I put them on my heart. "Don't worry," I told Momma. "I know how to get there."

PERMISSIONS

LAST DANCE
Words and Music by Paul Jabaru
© 1977 (Renewed 2005) EMI BLACKWOOD MUSIC and OLGA
MUSIC All Rights Controlled and Administered by EMI BLACK-
WOOD MUSIC INC. All Rights Reserved
International Copyright Secured   Used by Permission

LITTLE JAZZ BIRD
Music and lyrics by George Gershwin and Ira Gershwin
© 1924 (renewed) WB MUSIC CORP.
Lyrics Reprinted by Permission of ALFRED PUBLISHING CO., INC.
All Rights Reserved

Star of David on p. 213 used by permission of USHMM, courtesy of
Claudine Cerf. The views or opinions expressed in this book, and the
context in which theimages are used, do not necessarily reflect the views
or policy of, nor imply approval or endorsement by,
the United States Holocaust Memorial Museum.